PRIMAL

MEN OF CLUB TRISKELION

J.L. QUICK

PRIMAL COPYRIGHT
© 2024 by J.L. Quick Books LLC

All rights reserved. Printed in the United States of America. No part of this book may be used or reproduced in any manner whatsoever without the written permission except in the case of brief quotations embodied in critical articles or reviews.

This book is a work of fiction. Names, characters, businesses, organizations, places, events and incidents either are the product of the author's imagination or are used fictitiously. Any resemblance to actual persons, living or dead, events, or locales is entirely coincidental.

Cover Design: Spice Me Up Editing & Design (Jodi)
Editing: Spice Me Up Editing (Katie)

AUTHOR'S NOTE

This novel is a contemporary dark romance. It contains scenes and descriptive adult content, recommended for adult (18+) readers.

As a contemporary, dark romance work of fiction, this novel is not intended to be a portrayal of a healthy relationship or a 'how to guide' for the kink and lifestyle elements depicted within.

For those interested in exploring aspects of kink and/or dominant-submissive relationships explored in the following chapters, please do so responsibly and with appropriate reference materials.

TRIGGER WARNINGS

Violence

Gun Violence

Assault

Murder

Masturbation

Corruption Kink

Sexual Acts in a Church

Consensual Non-Consent Scenes

Oral Sex

Somnophilia

Blasphemy

Religious Degradation

Light Stalking

Voyeurism

Exhibitionism

Snowsleding

Threats of Incest (not by MMC or Family Members)

Threats of Sexual Assault (not by MMC)

Cuckholding/Hot-Wifing (On Page References)

Group Sex Scenes (not MMC or FMC)

Bondage (not MMC or FMC)

Sadistic/Pain Play (not MMC or FMC)

Heavy Impact Play (not MMC or FMC)

Pregnancy (not FMC)

Childbirth (not FMC)

TRIGGER WARNINGS

This novel may contain scenes and descriptive adult content that might be triggering for some readers.

GLOSSARY

This novel contains dialect commonly found in Ireland and Great Britain.

A stóirín — My little treasure

Cailín álainn — Beautiful girl

Cailín deas — Pretty girl

Daidi — Daddy

Fecked – drunk

Go hálainn – Beautiful

Mam — Mom/mother

Máthair chríonna — Grandmother

Mo ghrá — My Love

Piscín — Kitten

Póg mo thóin — Kiss my ass

Rud ar bith do mo dheartháir — Anything for my brother

Shite — shit

Take for a ride — Sex

Uncail — Uncle

Wanking off — Masturbating

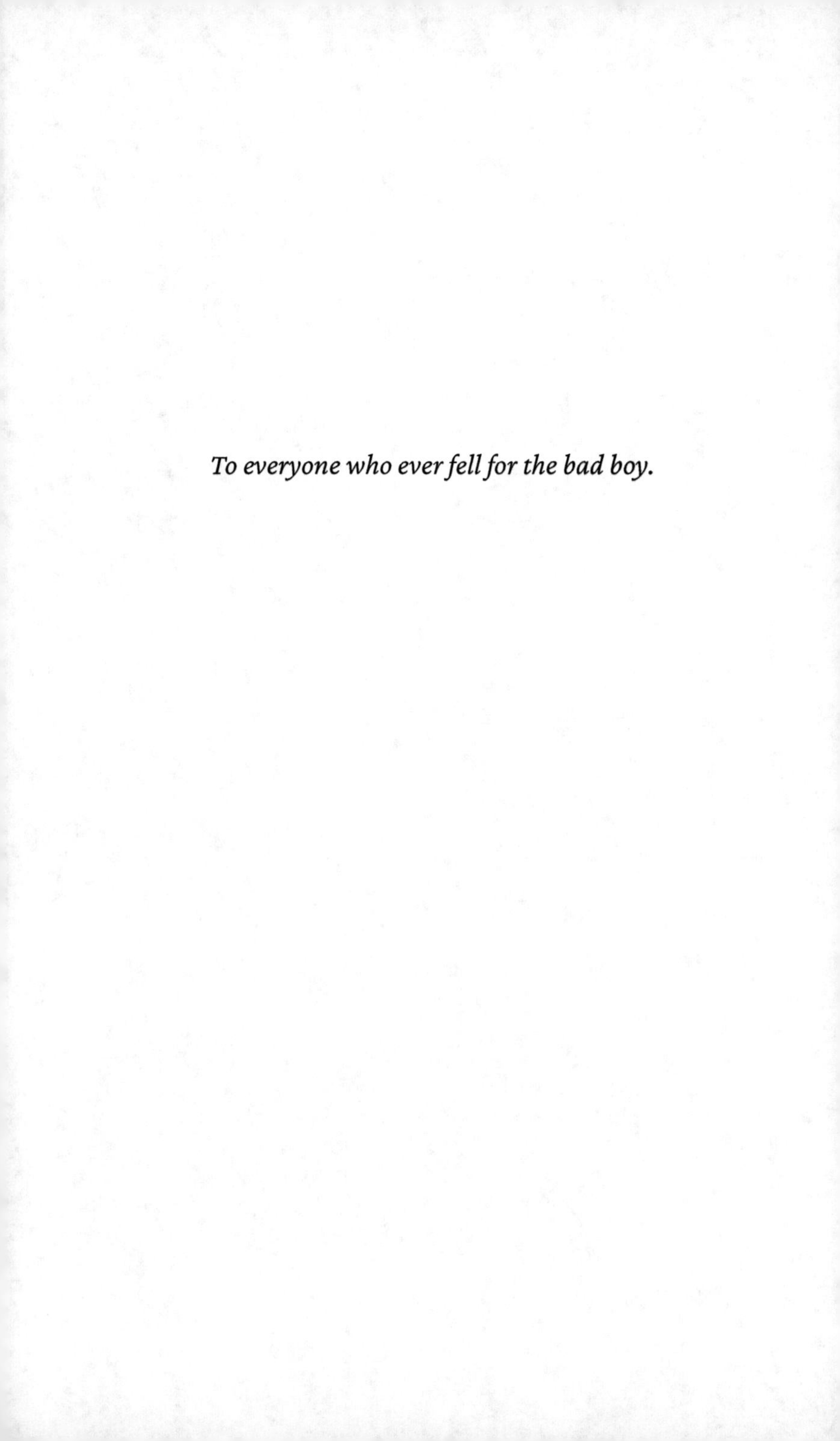

To everyone who ever fell for the bad boy.

...and you dirty little sinners who have thought about being unholy in church.

CHAPTER ONE
FINNIGAN

"Forgive me, Father, for I have sinned a fucking lot."

"Finnigan Shay Evans," Father O'Flaherty reprimands me from beyond the lattice screen separating our respective sides of the confessional. He doesn't hold back his annoyance. Not that he ever has. He has been very clear and honest about his—and God's—opinion of my frivolous lifestyle and questionable life choices for as long as I can remember. "Mind your tongue. You will not disrespect God—"

"Or your confessional," I condescendingly mock his tone as I finish his sentence with an eye roll. I've heard the words enough over the past twenty or so years to know, with certainty, that they were coming. Father O'Flaherty has admonished me with the exact phrase nearly every time I have stepped foot inside this confessional.

Probably all well-deserved.

Actually, definitely *all well-deserved.*

Kneeling on the worn, tufted green cushion with my elbows resting on the prayer ledge below the lattice screen, I breathe in the familiar woodsy scent as I continue my confession. "It has been two weeks since my last confession. In that time, I have repeatedly given in to my carnal desires, both with women… and myself. Both in quite plentiful amounts, actually."

"Do you feel remorseful?"

"No," I answer honestly. "Actually, I thoroughly enjoyed every last minute of it all. Anyone who tells you otherwise during their confession is either lying or doing it wrong. And considering the performance I gave Crystal and Diamond on Thursday, I'm actually feeling quite proud of myself. Not that any of the other nights of the week—or other women—were any less outstanding or memorable."

"Son, why do you come to confessional if you aren't going to take it seriously?"

My mam.

While my brothers may not attend mass or confessional as regularly as I do, *Mam* was determined to raise the five of us as devout Catholics. *Not that it has kept any of us on the straight and narrow.* She knew we would follow after our father into this life of depravity.

Which we all did. Eagerly. We all presume that church and confessional were her way of hoping we don't all burn in hell.

In *Mam's* eyes, we were always good boys at heart. She wasn't entirely wrong in her belief. Us Evans brothers live and breathe family values. There isn't a thing in this world we wouldn't do for one another or the people we bring into our family. We love hard. I just happen to share my love freely. *And really fucking often.*

"Carnal sin, impure thoughts, and pridefulness," Father O'Flaherty repeats my sins back to me. "I guess I should congratulate you for not taking a life this week."

He sure is a sarcastic and patronizing fuck for a priest.

At this point, I don't think there is much of anything I could say to surprise him. *He sure takes it in stride, though.* Father O'Flaherty has been taking my confessions since I was a teenager. Most weeks, he knows my confession before I have the opportunity to give it. It *is* the same week after week, with my debauchery and immorality—only growing since the *incident* with Missy O'Harrah—continuing to affirm his opinion of me. Fucking a handful—*or more*—of different women, getting *fecked*, more impure thoughts than I could possibly count, and lately killing at least a few men between visits to this little wooden box.

"About that..." I ignore his condescension. "It was a slow week, though. Only two men. And in my defense, one of them was a consequence of saving Tristan's life."

"While a small part of me wants to commend your admirable action of saving his life, I can't do so with good conscience, knowing that the decisions you and your brothers make put you in that position to start with."

Fair point.

"I would counsel or offer advice on how to mitigate your sins, Finnigan, but I am quite certain we both know that it would be a waste of both our time. Do you agree, son?"

"I'm a weak man, Father," I lament with a shrug.

Really fucking weak for a cailín deas.

"Ten Hail Marys, and please try to refrain from your sinful ways," Father O'Flaherty gives my penance. From his tone, it's clear we both know I won't be doing the latter.

"I'll do my best, Father," I respond, knowing damn well I will be racking up sins for my next confession by this evening. *I* wasn't the only one that had a good time with Crystal and Diamond earlier this week since they've both texted me twice now about getting together again this evening. I give my Act of Contrition and wait for Father O'Flaherty to provide my prayer of absolution. Once he finishes, I'll be free to walk from the confessional with a clean slate to start the new week.

When I place my hand on the knob of the confessional door, the cool metal turns in my palm and the door pulls open, revealing a gorgeous blonde on the other side.

"Oh! I'm so sorry," she gasps upon nearly joining me in the booth. More words come from her, but I'm so mesmerized by her pouty pink lips and the sparkling emerald flecks in her hazel eyes that I don't comprehend them.

"*Go hálainn,*" I exhale. Even with her modest attire, there is no mistaking the body hiding beneath it. The well-fitted cream blouse she's wearing does nothing to conceal the swell of her perky tits. My eyes continue to rake down her body to the tartan pencil skirt hugging her voluptuous hips and thighs.

Plaid fucking skirts are my kryptonite.

She's so fucking stunning that I'm practically salivating over her. Every thought racing through my mind involves learning if she's as demure in what she's wearing underneath that blouse and skirt.

Welp, there's one sin for next week's confession.

Here's hoping she leads to at least five more.

CHAPTER TWO
CATLIN

The man towering over me looks nothing like any of the men I have ever seen in church before. His broad stature alone is intimidating as he stares down at me, but it is nothing compared to how menacing-looking the rest of him is. His eyes are light blue, but there is a wild, untamed darkness looming behind them.

I've seen plenty of men with tattoos before, but no one like him. *At least, not in person.* His chiseled face is the only skin I can see that isn't covered with them. Ink covers the back of his hands and fingers, with the same geometric pattern swirling from under the collar of his shirt and up his neck. It stops just below his rugged jawline but continues along the shaved sides of his head, coming to a well-defined stop at the edge of his meticulously coiffed dark-brown hair.

I take a few steps backward to put distance between

the two of us as I continue to apologize, "I didn't realize anyone was in ther—"

"Nothing to apologize for, sweetheart." His deep voice has a gravelly tone that only adds to his already gruff demeanor. I swallow hard as he tries to close what little distance I have put between us. As I continue to take small steps backward, he repeatedly advances like we're playing a game of cat and mouse. A smug smile tugs at the corner of his mouth, and his tongue slowly drags along his lower lip as he stalks toward me like I'm his prey. When his smile spreads, it is quite clear that he's enjoying this.

"Catlin, why don't you go wait in my office?" Uncle Sean's voice startles me. I suddenly find myself relieved that we aren't alone and curious of how this little game was going to play out. His voice deepens and carries a sternness I've never heard from him as he turns his attention to the man standing before me. "Finnigan Evans, I think it's time you be on your way." It isn't a question. Uncle Sean is telling him to leave, politely.

Finnigan's demeanor doesn't falter. He holds his ground, standing only a few inches away from me, as his powder-blue eyes bore into mine. "I'll see you next week, Father," he politely replies to Uncle Sean without pulling his gaze from me. Lowering his voice and dipping his head slightly, he whispers, "Hopefully you too, sweetheart."

The smug smile spreads into a full grin, and he gives me a cheeky wink. It isn't until he steps around me that I realize my heart is racing and I have forgotten how to breathe. Sucking in a breath as he passes, I inhale his spicy amber-and-vanilla-scented cologne. It lingers in the air for a moment as he walks between the pews behind me.

Breathing in the fading scent, my eyes trail the man walking toward the exit as I compose myself. Still on edge, I jump slightly when Uncle Sean lightly grasps my arm. "Are you okay, Catlin?"

"Um... Yeah... Yes," I stammer. "He just startled me. That's all." *Just a little scared.* He just frightened me a bit, clearly evident by the pounding of my heart against my rib cage.

"I told you I would have picked you up at Penn Station." Uncle Sean pulls me in for a welcoming hug before lightly scolding me, "New York City isn't quite the same as Galway."

"Clearly!" I exclaim as I arch a brow. Garnering a quick glance toward the back of the church, I find the heavily tattooed man has left. "I didn't expect—"

"Most of my congregation are not like him..." Uncle Sean shakes his head.

"You mean... the tattoos?" I ask.

He nods. "Among many other things. The rest are great families and upstanding people."

"Oh…" I softly exhale, realizing he is subtly letting me know that Finnegan and his family is not the type of family to be seen with.

Before I have a chance to say anything further or ask any of the thousands of questions swirling through my thoughts, Uncle Sean grabs my suitcase from beside the pew. Lifting the heavy bag, he grunts, "Let me show you where you'll be staying."

I follow him past the altar and into the back of the church. We walk through a small courtyard filled with flowers and what appears to be a tiny vegetable garden, surrounded by a tall brick wall, toward a small brick home. After opening the door and gesturing for me to enter, Uncle Sean shares, "It isn't proper for you to stay in the rectory with me. This used to be a small convent, but it hasn't been used in a few years."

"It's perfect," I exclaim, stepping through the threshold. The modest space is minimally decorated, housing nothing more than a navy couch—that looks well beyond second-hand use—and a couple of end tables with decade-old brass lamps and dusty shades. Anything would be perfect if it means I get to be back on this side of the ocean again.

I was shipped to Galway—*against my will*—when I was fourteen upon the untimely passing of my parents. They had named my Uncle Sean as my guardian, apparently not taking into account that a man of the cloth isn't exactly in the ideal situation for raising a teenage girl. Thinking it was for the best, he sent me to Galway to live with *máthair chríonna* while I finished my high school education at an all-girls secondary school.

"It's temporary," I remind him.

"Very," he agrees. "We agreed on six months while you fill in for my parish secretary."

"I know," I huff. I hate that I lied to get here, but he never would've let me come had he known I had accepted enrollment at NYU. "And then I'm getting my butt back on a plane to Galway to start the spring semester at university."

CHAPTER THREE
FINNIGAN

FINNIGAN

My phone buzzes in the front pocket of my jeans. I pull it out and swipe open the waiting text message, and I'm met with two quite remarkable sets of perky tits.

CRYSTAL

If you aren't here in twenty minutes, we're starting without you.

These two are definitely persistent.

"*Uncail* Finn!" the demanding little preschooler I promised to babysit tonight shouts from the landing. "You're supposed to be getting ready to go swimming."

Sorry, ladies. Enjoy yourselves.

DIAMOND

> You DO realize what you're passing
> up, right?

The image that follows her text would make some porn stars blush, and I'm suddenly left feeling a little less than adequate. *Definitely not a feeling I'm used to in that department.*

Already dressed in her lime-green, floral bathing suit and matching hot-pink pool floaties, Fiona stares up at me with her big blue eyes as she tugs at my jeans and pleads, "C'mon."

> Based on that photo, the two of you
> will be just fine without me.

> Besides, a feisty little redhead has
> demanded my undivided attention this
> evening, and she definitely isn't taking
> no for an answer.

Without another thought, I turn off my phone, toss it onto the couch, and kneel on the ground before Fiona. "You're awfully demanding for a little peanut who was supposed to be in bed fifteen minutes ago."

"You promised," she huffs as I stand. With that adorable protruding lower lip, I couldn't recant on my commitment if I wanted to.

"I did. And what have I taught you about promises?" I kick off my shoes and pull my T-shirt over my head.

She thinks for a moment before exclaiming, "Evans always keep their promises!"

"That's right, peanut." I throw my shirt on top of my phone and begin running toward the patio as I shout, "Last one in is a rotten egg."

"You can't swim in your pants!" Fiona's giggles follow behind me as I pretend to race her to the pool.

"Watch me!" I scoop her into my arms and cannonball us both into the warm water.

When we push through the surface, Fiona swipes her matted red locks from her face and blows the water from her lips over my face as she squeals, "Again!"

Balling her in my arms, I toss her across the pool until even *I'm* tired. She wraps her floaty-covered arms around my neck and places a big, wet chlorine kiss against my cheek. "You're gonna be a really good *daidi*, *Uncail* Finn."

A dad? She can't be serious.

Fiona's sentiment is sweet, but I'm pretty sure I tap out at fun uncle.

"Really, Finnigan?" Quinn scoffs from the doorway to the patio as Declan glares at me from behind her.

"I think your dad is going to disagree with you, peanut." I spin her onto my back and make sure her hands are wrapped snuggly around my neck.

I hold Fiona's hands tightly and swim her to the edge of the pool as she teases, "You're in so much trouble."

We reach the edge, where Declan is waiting with a very disappointed scowl. He pulls her from the water and up to his chest as he quips, "And so are you, *a stóirín*. I am pretty sure *you* should've been in bed a couple of hours ago."

The moment she snickers as he carries her inside, I quickly realize that I'm the only one who is going to be receiving a lecture about letting her take a late-night swim.

Quinn firmly slaps a navy beach towel against my chest as I climb from the pool. "I expect you to spoil her, Finn, but you can't keep her up this late. I'm starting to think you actually enjoy riling him up until he wants to beat the piss out of you."

"Shhh." I smirk, drying my hair and arms as I follow her back toward the house. "It'll be our secret."

Quinn stops abruptly at the doorway, "Pants, Finn. You are soaked. You aren't coming in here and leaving puddles all over my floors."

My heavy, wet jeans are plastered to my legs and leave a massive puddle around my feet. "Fine," I huff as I undo the button and lower the zipper. Quinn turns her back to me as I begin the struggle of peeling myself out of the wet denim. Tossing my soaked jeans and boxer briefs on the patio beside her, I tease, "You know, if you wanted me naked, Quinn, all you had to do is ask."

"For fuck's sake," Declan groans from the far side of the living room as I wrap the towel Quinn gave me around my waist. "Do you need to constantly hit on my wife?"

I stare at him for a moment before raking my eyes over Quinn. It's intended to be playful, but there is no denying how fucking gorgeous she is with her rapidly growing belly. Pregnancy definitely suits her. Wrapping my arms around her from behind, I rub my hands over her swollen stomach and place a kiss against her cheek before responding to him. "You probably should've married an ugly woman instead of this MILF. Because if she wasn't your wife..."

"Finnigan," Declan snarls, and I can't quite gauge his level of seriousness.

"What is it you lot always say? Rud ar bith do mo dheartháir?" Quinn chimes with a chuckle, placing her hand over mine. "Besides, it's not like he would knock me up."

"Pretty sure I'm not the only one that enjoys riling him up," I whisper against her ear, causing her to let out a loud cackle.

"Do not fucking encourage him," Declan growls as he pulls Quinn from my embrace and holds her possessively close.

"Relax, old man. We're just pushing your buttons. A blind man could see that Quinn Evans only has eyes for you."

CHAPTER FOUR
CATLIN

Having finished the Callaghan baptism programs for tomorrow and the time being so close to lunch, I head down to the nave in search of Uncle Sean to let him know I'm heading out for a little while.

After mass last weekend, I met a wonderful pregnant woman. She lived just outside Dublin for a few years but had visited Galway quite often. The two of us clicked immediately and made plans for lunch today. She should be getting here any time now. When I reach the narthex, I find she has already arrived. She's talking to a well-built man standing with his back to me, and her sleepy little girl is resting her head on his shoulder.

"Catlin." A broad smile spreads over her face as she waves me over.

"Hey, Quinn." I wave as I approach. "This must be your husb—"

My words catch in my throat when he turns and I find myself face-to-face with the heavily tattooed man I bumped into a week ago.

"I wish." He flashes a devilish grin at Quinn.

She playfully swats at his arm. "Catlin just met me. I really don't need her thinking I'm sleeping with my husband's brothers."

"*Brother*, because I wouldn't be willing to share you. And no one said a thing about sleeping," he teases.

She shakes her head with a smile. "Catlin, have you had the pleasure of meeting my relentless flirt of a brother-in-law?"

"Briefly," he answers for me, a coy smile pulling at the corners of his mouth. "But definitely not for long enough."

"The two of you are going to have a few more minutes to get acquainted then because I have to pee every five minutes these days," Quinn excuses herself.

"We haven't *officially* met." He shuffles his hold on the sleeping little girl in his arms and outstretches his ink-covered hand. "I'm Finnigan Evans. Or Finn."

Slipping my hand into his, a sensation like goose-bumps—without the chill—travels up my arm. He squeezes it gently as I struggle to remember my name. "C-Catlin."

"You're new here, right?" As he continues to hold my hand, his thumb leisurely dragging along my skin. "I've been attending this church my whole life, and I know all the *cailín deas* that come here."

"I bet you do," I quip, pulling my palm from his.

"But definitely none pretty as you." He softly exhales as his gaze lingers on mine before glancing down my body.

I've met plenty of men like Finnigan. Older men flirting with younger women like me are only interested in one thing. *At least that's what máthair chríonna would always say.* That *one thing* definitely isn't happening. Not with him. Not with anyone. Well, at least not until I'm married. Or at least until I'm with the man who plans to marry me.

That has to be good enough for God, right?

"Something tells me that I am definitely not the first girl you've said that to," I snidely respond. "Probably not even the first one today."

"Yeah." He smirks, silently acknowledging the accuracy of my observation. With honest eyes and a sincere tone, he confesses, "But you, beautiful, are the first one I actually meant it to."

Warm crimson creeps up my neck and over my cheeks. I drop my gaze to the floor, so I'm not looking him in the eyes when he realizes the effect he just had on me. Even with my eyes focused on the tiled floor beneath my feet, I know his heated gaze is still on my flushed cheeks.

"I'm so sorry. These babies and my bladder are fighting for space, and my bladder is definitely not winning." Quinn returns, breaking the awkward silence. "Can you help get Fiona into the car?"

"I'm done giving Father O'Flaherty his heart attack for the week." Finn chuckles. "Let me take her so you two can enjoy your lunch."

"Are you sure?" Quinn asks.

"Always. I'll steal your car seat and take my little peanut over to the club. You and Rory can swing by after your lunch to pick her up."

She stretches up onto her toes and places a kiss on his cheek. "Thank you."

With Fiona in one arm, Finnigan uses his other to hold open the church door for the two of us to exit. As he walks with her toward a sleek black sports car, he gestures toward a tall red-headed man standing near the black Tahoe parked beside him. The man reaches into the SUV and climbs out with a car seat in hand, which he promptly installs into the backseat of Finn's car.

"Is your husband joining us for lunch?" I ask.

"Rory?" Her voice ticks up in confusion, and I give a quick nod. "He's not my husband."

"Oh," I murmur as I climb into the backseat of the Tahoe.

After sliding in behind me, she clarifies, "Rory works for my husband and his brothers."

"Like your driver?"

"And then some." Quinn reaches between the seats and gives his arm a tender squeeze. "But he's like family. Isn't that right, Rory?"

"Yes, ma'am." He smiles at her in the rearview.

"We've talked about this," she teasingly scolds him. "After all we've been through, you get to call me Quinn."

We make casual small talk as Rory drives us to a little café a few miles from the church. "You had said you were having a hard time meeting people, so I hope you don't mind, but I invited a couple of people to join us."

"I don't mind at all!" I exclaim. "I've been here a little over a week and you are literally the only person I know besides Uncle Sean."

While I love Uncle Sean to pieces, it would be nice to have someone just a tad closer to my age to spend some time with.

CHAPTER FIVE
FINNIGAN

"Where the fuck have you been?" Declan snarls as I walk into the lounge of the club, not realizing I have Fiona in tow.

"Really?" I nudge the still-sleepy Fiona walking beside me. "You don't yell at him for saying that?"

Still groggy from her nap in the car, Fiona merely shrugs.

"*A stóirín*, what are you doing with Uncle Finn? Where's Quinn?" Declan asks, his tone noticeably softer with Fiona than me.

"I dunno," she mumbles through her yawning stretch.

"I offered to watch my peanut while Quinn went to lunch with this *cailín deas* I would like to take for a ride." I wink at him, a smile spreading across my face when my thoughts momentarily drift back toward Catlin.

I usually have gorgeous women on my mind, but Catlin has been the primary source of my thoughts from the moment I met her. She's barely left my mind since leaving the church. The feel of her soft, porcelain skin isn't the only thing I'm thinking about. *Although that also seems to keep creeping in.* As a rich and powerful Evans brother, women practically fall at my feet. But not her. She sees right through my flirtatious bullshit and wants nothing to do with it.

And fuck, do I ever love a challenge.

"You mean Father O'Flaherty's niece?" he clarifies with an arched brow.

"No. Catlin," I correct him. "The gorgeous-as-hell new parish secretary."

Repeating himself and shaking his head, Declan insists, "Father O'Flaherty's niece. You absolutely will *not* be having a repeat of the Missy O'Harrah incident with Father's niece. That would get us all banned from Our Lady of Grace and you know it."

"Grow up." I scoff, my upper lip curling in annoyance. I cover Fiona's ears with my hands before continuing, "I'm way too old to be finger-banging women in church. I'm not a horny teenager anymore. I'm a gentleman. I'd take her home first."

Declan rolls his eyes and lets out a fatherly sigh. I drop my hands from Fiona's ears as Liam joins us, laughing. "No. You're just a horny thirty-two-year-old."

An innocent laugh erupts beside me, and Fiona chimes, "*Uncail* Finn doesn't have horns."

"And I think that's about enough of this conversation for you." Liam swoops Fiona off the floor and into his arms, mouthing *"sorry"* to Declan. Swaying her in his embrace, he carries her toward the door. "How about you help me grab a box from my car so your dad can murder Uncle Finn without any witnesses?"

"Piss the old man off even more and then take the only person keeping him from exploding at me. Thanks a lot, Li."

Declan stares at me; his brows furrowed with a disapproving scowl as Liam takes Fiona out of earshot. In turn, I stare back at him in complete disbelief.

O'Flaherty's niece? That gorgeous woman couldn't possibly be related to that stuffy old fart.

"No," Declan firmly scolds me. "Absolutely not."

Raising my voice, I roll my eyes and snark, "Seriously? Are you going to ground me if I don't do as you say, Dad? Will I need to go to my room?"

"I'm fucking serious, Finn!" Declan's voice booms louder than mine.

He knows I despise being told what to do. Or, in this case, what I can't do. "What are you going to do to stop me, old man?" I step toward him, snarling.

Squaring up to me and fully prepared to beat the shit out of me, he spits, "You will not—"

"What the fuck are the two of you arguing about?" Tristan storms into the lounge from the hallway, interrupting our near sparring match.

"Finn's inability to not put his cock where he shouldn't," Declan snaps.

Tristan's head snaps toward me, his eyes wide and curious. "Quinn? You fucking didn—"

"I fucking wish." I smirk at Declan, knowing it'll piss him off.

"If he'd fucked my wife, we'd be having a *very* different conversation," Declan informs Tristan as the heat of his rage visibly washes over his face. "I would've fucking killed him." I wholeheartedly believe him. Declan would have no qualms about ending any man that dared lay a hand on her. As much as I playfully flirt with Quinn, that's all it is: a playful flirtation. I would never cross that line.

At least not with any of my brother's wives.

Tristan wedges himself between the two of us and pushes. "It's not like you have a favorite stripper for him to fuck. He didn't fuck Quinn. So, what the hell is the issue?"

"Finn has his eyes on Father O'Flaherty's niece," Declan answers.

"Are you trying to get us fucking excommunicated?" Tristan chuckles as he glances at me.

"Have you fucking seen her?" I exclaim. "Excommunication would be well worth those long legs wrapped around my head or those pouty, pink lips around my cock."

"For fuck's sake, Finn," Declan declares. "Even if she wasn't related to O'Flaherty, she's practically jailbait. And way too fucking young for you!"

"Then I'll be in good fucking company with Tristan," I retort. "Or do I need to remind you how much younger than him *his* wife is?"

"Layla was *not* jailbait," Tristan huffs, displeased with my accusation.

"And neither is Catlin," I snap, even though part of me knows Declan isn't entirely wrong. *Not that I would ever admit that to him.* She can't be much older than twenty; at least a decade—if not more—younger than me. I fuck twenty-year-olds all the damn time, and Declan hasn't had an issue with any of them. He only has a problem with *her.*

"She's not the girl for you, Finn." Declan softens his tone, taking a different approach. "I've met her. She is nothing like the girls you normally date."

"I don't *only* date strippers, you know?" I huff in annoyance.

Declan shifts his weight, clearly trying to choose his next words wisely. "She's not the kind of girl you take for dinner or drinks and then bring home to fuck. She's a good girl, Finnigan."

I bet she is...

CHAPTER SIX
CATLIN

After a short drive, we reach a quaint little restaurant and pull to a stop behind another SUV with all the windows blacked out. There are two men with a similar muscular build to Rory waiting on the sidewalk beside it. With their plain, non-well-fitted dress slacks and button-down shirts, they nearly blend in with the pedestrians passing them on the sidewalk— minus the guns affixed to their hips. They both respectfully tip their heads at Quinn as we pass them on our way to the entrance.

Did I not realize she's famous or something?

Holding the door for us to enter the cafe, Rory informs Quinn, "I'll be just outside with Grady and Raegan if you need anything."

"Do you boys want lunch?" she kindly asks.

"No, thank you, ma—" He abruptly pauses when he catches himself. "Quinn."

This place kind of reminds me of a little coffee shop I would sometimes go to in Galway to study. The street-facing side of the building is almost entirely paned windows, letting in a ton of natural sunlight for the copious amounts of greenery scattered throughout the interior. There are small conversation areas created with wicker tables and chairs, all with views of the street.

Following Quinn, we make our way to a table toward the back, where a man and a woman, not much older than me, are waiting. Reaching the table, Quinn introduces me. "Catlin, this is my sister-in-law, Layla."

"Wow, mama!" the man exclaims. "You're as big as a house."

Layla smacks him and Quinn sighs, "And this, for some reason, is our friend, Jorge."

"Nice to meet you both." I chuckle as I take a seat between Layla and Quinn. "So, are *you* married to Finn?"

"To Finn? God, no." Layla scoffs. "I'm married to Tristan."

Joining in her laughter, Jorge chimes, "But he wishes."

"Oh, hush," Quinn teasingly admonishes them before

turning her attention toward me. "Don't pay them any mind. Finnigan is a salacious flirt."

"Yeah… I picked up on that," I quip with a coy smile.

"Can I take your drink order? Perhaps some appetizers," the server interrupts us when he approaches the table.

"We'll have a bottle of rosé." Jorge gestures between him and Layla. "Or do you not like rosé, Catlin?"

"Oh. Um, I can't," I stammer. "I'll actually just have sparkling water."

"Same. And the biggest basket of fried pickles you can find," Quinn gives her order, causing Layla to chuckle. "I swear, it's not a pregnancy thing. I'm just starving and they're so good."

"Fried pickles are delicious," I agree when the server walks from our table.

"Pickles. No rosé." Jorge eyes me suspiciously for a moment before asking, "Are you pregnant too, sweetie?"

"Goodness, no." I shake my head. "I'm not married. And no to the wine because I'm not old enough to drink."

"You do know you don't have to be married to be pregnant, right?" Jorge teases, causing my cheeks to match the contents of the bottle of wine being placed on the table.

"Jorge!" Layla lightly smacks his arm. "Behave. Not everyone is as welcoming of having strange men in their bed as you."

"Or you." He cockily arches a brow. "Finding Mr. Right isn't going well, so I'm settling for Mr. Right Now, Mr. Later Tonight, and Mr. What Are You Doing Tomorrow."

"Oh…" I blurt.

"I've given up all hope for Conor." Jorge lets out a heavy sigh. "That man and all his muscles seem to be steadfast in the hetero-normative lane."

My brows furrow in confusion. "Conor?"

"So, you've met Finn. He's the baby," Layla begins to clarify. "Quinn is married to his eldest brother, Declan. Me to the next oldest, Tristan. Conor and Liam fall between him and Finn."

"Are they all—"

"Absolutely fucking gorgeous?" Jorge interrupts me. "Girl, yes!"

"What about you?" Quinn shakes her head at Jorge. "Are you seeing anyone? Or were you in Galway?"

"No. Uncle Sean had me enrolled at an all-girls boarding school, which was pretty much a step below a convent. And my *máthair chríonna* was quite strict about things like curfew when I wasn't at school. I've been on a date here and there, but that's really about it."

"So, you're a virg—"

"Jorge!" Layla's voice rises a few octaves as she slaps Jorge's arm again before turning her attention to me. "I apologize for him. His mother didn't raise him with any manners."

"I'm sorry." Jorge rolls his eyes and feigns an apology. "It's not every day you meet someone as gorgeous as you, in their twenties, who's never... you know."

"Well, I'm not twenty yet." I shrug. "At least not until Tuesday. And thank you."

Jorge scrunches his face over his glass of wine. "For what?"

"The compliment." I blush.

"Seriously?" he asks. "Have you seen you? Even *I'd* have sex with you."

"Gee, thanks." I laugh.

The four of us chat throughout lunch. Even with how different I am to the three of them, I have the most fun I've had since arriving in New York City. They are so welcoming, authentic, and real. *Especially Jorge, who literally says whatever is on his mind.* The time spent with the them passes too quickly, and before I know it, we're all walking toward the waiting SUVs parked along the sidewalk.

Jorge hugs me as we make our goodbyes. "My offer stands."

"Thanks, but I think I'm going to pass." I chuckle against his chest, declining his proposal to find a man to get me *devirginized* before my birthday.

"We'll see you next week for your birthday lunch." Layla hugs me and places a soft kiss on my cheek.

"Absolutely." I squeeze her back, feeling like I'm hugging an old friend instead of a someone I met a few hours ago.

I thank Quinn during the short ride back to the church, grateful to have met some people I truly look forward to spending more time with.

"You are so welcome." She reaches across the seat to hug me as we approach the church. "I'll text you about next week."

Rory opens my door, and as I slide from the Tahoe, I notice Uncle Sean talking with a member of the congregation by the front door of the church. The SUV's door shutting draws his attention, and I'm immediately met with his disapproving stare. I can vaguely overhear him excusing himself from his conversation as I approach. He is immediately on my heels as I hastily walk through the church toward the courtyard.

CHAPTER SEVEN
CATLIN

"Catlin O'Flaherty," Uncle Sean sternly calls, following me as I make my way through the church. Ignoring him, I step into the hallway, running behind the altar, and continue toward my residence.

"Catlin Aine O'Flaherty!" he shouts this time as I shove through the doors into the courtyard. His tone, reprimanding me like a child, causes my feet to cement in place. Standing just beyond the threshold, I contemplate letting the heavy door slip from my fingers to make a barrier between us. Instead, I close my eyes and let out a deep breath before turning to face him with a faux-smile.

His brows are lowered, and his lips are tightly pursed, accentuating his firmly disapproving scowl. The gaze boring through me carries the same condemnation. He's angry. Furious, even.

"I don't want you associating with *those* people, Catlin," he declaims.

"Those people?" I exclaim. "*Those* people—Quinn, Layla, and Jorge—are the first nice people I've met since I got here."

"I have tried to be subtle about it, but you don't seem to understand," he lectures. "You don't know who they really are. They are not good people. I don't want you around them."

Rolling my eyes, I huff. "That's very Christian of you, **Father O'Flaherty**."

"Don't sass me, Catlin," he snips.

"Then stop treating me like a child." I cross my arms and stare back at him.

"Then stop acting like one." He scoffs. "You are an employee of this church—and my niece—how you live your life is a representation of our beliefs and teachings. I will not allow you to associate with those... *sinners*. The lot of them are nothing but murderers, thieves, and seductresses."

Seductresses? He can't be serious. My new friends from lunch might be—or have been—a little adventurous with their sex lives, but so were at least half the girls I went to boarding school with.

But murderers?

Clearly, he's not referring to the three wonderful people I spent my afternoon with. There's just no way. Of the rest of them, I've only met Finn. Sure, he's a total flirt… But a killer? He seems so… sweet.

"Are you listening to me, Catlin?" Uncle Sean snarls, noticing my lack of attention to his rambling. "You aren't to spend time with them."

"You're serious?"

"Deadly," he confirms. "I expect you to be pleasant and cordial with them inside the confines of this church—where it's safe—but I don't want you seeing them beyond these walls."

Arching an inquisitive brow, I ask, "Where it's safe?"

"They don't bring their troubles in here. I don't worry about anything happening to you in here, but I can't say the same out there." Uncle Sean's demeanor relaxes, and there's a bit of softness in his previously anger-filled gaze. His pained words catch in his throat, "You don't know what kind of danger you're putting yourself in being seen with them in public, and I can't risk losing you. My brother would never forgive me."

"Uncle Sean…" I softly exhale as he closes the distance between us and pulls me into an embrace; it's so tight that it feels like he's trying to never let me go. "You aren't going to lose me."

"I know you aren't a little girl anymore"—his words vibrate against the top of my head—"but I'm begging you to listen to me on this. Stay away from the Evans family."

As he continues to squeeze me tightly, I know he's waiting for me to acknowledge his request. But it's a promise I can't quite bring myself to give him. These are the first people I've met since getting here who actually welcomed me into their tight-knit group.

The first people ever actually.

I'm not quite ready to let that go.

Releasing me from his suffocating embrace, he urges, "Can you promise me that?"

No... I can't.

"Catlin?" he presses.

Not wanting to lie—or upset him—I give the only answer I can muster. "Uh-huh."

"You always were such a good girl." He smiles down at me with pride. "Your parents would both be so proud of the woman you're becoming. I know I am."

That's me...

Always the good girl; following the rules and doing exactly what is asked and expected of me. What I want is always to be an afterthought so that I don't upset

Uncle Sean, *Máthair Chríonna*, or even the sisters who ran the boarding school.

Leisurely walking through the courtyard to the convent, I can't help but think about it more. Pushing to move to New York is the first time I've ever actually made a decision for me. It's the *only* selfish choice I've ever made. My phone dinging in my purse drags me from thoughts. I pull it out to find a few text messages.

QUINN

I made reservations for the four of us.
Tuesday at six.

LAYLA

Sounds good!

JORGE

And if you change your mind…

My thumbs linger over the screen as I weigh my conversation with Uncle Sean. It's lunch with a few people I connect with. *How bad can being friends with them actually be?*

Looking forward to it!

JORGE

Yes, girl! I am going to get to wingman
the fuck out of you this weekend!

The dinner! I mean about the dinner!

LAYLA

Pretty sure you just absolutely crushed him. LOL.

Sorry, Jorge.

JORGE

It's fine. I'll just cry into my rosé

Or the hairy muscular chest of my date tonight.

"Gross," I mutter at the thought of my face being pressed into a hairy chest as I set my things on the table and shake my head.

Uncle Sean isn't going to like this. Not one bit.

CHAPTER EIGHT
FINNIGAN

"*Uncail* Finn!" Fiona screams my name in greeting as I walk through the front door. She's so excited, you'd think she hadn't seen me in weeks. She barrels through the living room in her princess pajamas and jumps into my arms.

Catching her, I grunt, "Hi peanut."

"Did you come to take me swimming?" she whispers.

"Are you trying to get me into trouble?" I tease. "I'm here to pick up your dad."

"He's upstairs getting dressed," she informs me as I carefully place her on the floor.

"*A stóirín*," Declan calls down the stairs. "Is there a reason you aren't in bed?"

Her lips purse, and her eyes widen when she realizes

she's in trouble. Giving her a playful tap, I urge, "You better get that cute little butt of yours upstairs."

"Good night, *Uncail* Finn."

"How was lunch the other day?" I ask Quinn as I walk into the kitchen.

"Finnigan Evans," she draws out my name and smirks. "Are you interested in my fried pickles and cheeseburger or the pretty blonde I caught you flirting with?"

Placing a chaste kiss on her cheek, I wink. "Definitely the pickles. You know I only have eyes for you, Quinn."

"Mmm-hmm," she quips with a knowing smile.

Grabbing a bar stool and saddling up to the counter, I huff. "Are you really going to make me ask?"

"No. But I'll tell you now, Finn, she's not one of your little one-night-stands." Quinn crosses her arms, and they rest slightly on her belly before she drops them onto the white granite of the island to lean closer to me. "If that's your interest in her, just walk away."

Why does everyone assume I'm incapable of anything other than a one-night-stand?

"I'm serious, Finnigan. She's a good Catholic girl," Quinn advises.

"For fuck's sake! I date more than strippers." I exclaim.

"Jesus Christ," Declan announces as he joins us. "Are we back on the O'Flaherty girl *again*?"

"I get it," Quinn acknowledges my interest. "She is absolutely fucking gorgeous."

Cocking a brow, I ask, "How didn't I know you had an interest in women?"

"I don—"

"Shhhh." I reach across the counter and press my finger to her lips to silence her. "Don't ruin this future wet dream for me."

Declan snakes his arm around my throat, pulling me away from Quinn and the barstool as he tightens the headlock. "While I'm more than certain you do it, I do not need to hear about you wanking off to my wife."

Pulling at Declan's arm, we scuffle across the kitchen floor. His forearm pulls more against my windpipe, and I struggle to breathe. I sweep my leg around his and topple us both to the floor with a thud. Declan quickly takes the upper hand, rolling onto his back and ensnaring me with both of his legs, rendering me practically unable to move. I slap my hand against his forearm, tapping out, but he doesn't lament.

"Let him go," Quinn sighs, rolling her eyes. "At some point, the lot of you are going to need to learn you aren't teenagers anymore, right?"

Releasing his grip, Declan shoves me from on top of him. I lay with the cool tiles against my back and struggle to catch my breath as Declan climbs from the floor beside me. Like the big brother he is, he stands over me and gently nudges me with his foot. "Let's go. We have somewhere to be."

Reluctantly, I roll onto my stomach and push myself from the floor before climbing to my feet. I fix my clothes as Declan kisses Quinn goodbye. Quinn rounds the island when Declan leaves us to grab his jacket. She lightly fists the front of my shirt, and her eyes are filled with worry when she looks up at me. "You make sure he gets home safe," she demands.

"Always." I place my hands over hers. Gripping the right one, I pull it from my shirt and place it on her stomach. "I promise you, that man is going to live a long life so he can watch Fiona, these babies, and that baseball team he still intends to impregnate you with grow up."

The worry lines on her face soften, and a small smile tugs at the corner of her mouth. Pressing onto her toes, she wraps her arms around my neck and places a soft kiss against my cheek as she whispers, "Thank you."

"I couldn't lose him. I don't enjoy annoying my other brothers nearly as much," I jest.

Quinn lets out a timid laugh as she lowers herself to her feet. Still lightly fisting my shirt with one hand, she imparts, "She'd be good for you, but she's sweet and innocent, Finn. You'll absolutely ruin her if you're just looking for a frivolous fling. So, choose what you decide to do wisely... For her sake."

Quinn is not naïve about my love life. *More correctly, my sex life.* For the past decade, my romantic encounters have been nothing more than a series of one-night-stands, an occasional situationship, and one very short-lived—*dull as fuck*—moment of monogamy.

"If you're done making out with my wife, can we get going?" Declan gruffs from the doorway.

Quinn calls after me as I cross the room to join Declan, "I'm serious, Finn."

"Understood." I nod.

So am I...

CHAPTER NINE
FINNIGAN

"About fucking time." Conor huffs as he climbs into my Bronco. "What took you guys so long?"

"Finn was busy trying to fuck my wife… again," Declan answers before I have a chance.

"*Actually*, the old man wasn't ready when I went to pick him up," I correct him.

Pulling back into traffic, the bottles in the crate at Conor's feet clatter against one another. "Fuck, Finn. Is there a reason you have"—he pauses to count—"a case with ten Molotov cocktails in the backseat?"

"Twelve seemed like too many." I laugh. "And you never know when they're going to come in handy."

"Are we sure *Mam* didn't drop him on his head when he was little?" Conor asks Declan.

Declan chuckles his response. "I wonder that every fucking day."

The two of them continue to bust my chops as we drive toward tonight's job. Considering it's nothing more than debt collection, the carful of us seems like overkill. When we pull up to the address Tristan provided, I park before what has to be at least a ten-million-dollar brownstone. Looking between my brothers, I ask, "Are we sure this is the right place?"

"Yup. Rich-as-fuck famous bloke that likes to"—Conor rolls his eyes and air quotes—"live dangerously with his illegal betting."

"Seriously?"

"It's why there's three of us," Declan informs me. "He has an entourage of muscle."

Yes!

It's been a dull-as-fuck week. I haven't hit or fucked anyone, and if I don't scratch one of those itches soon, I quite possibly might explode. "Grab my bat," I instruct Conor as the three of us climb from the SUV. Rounding the Bronco and stepping onto the curb, he tosses me my favorite intimidation tool.

A tall, burly man steps outside as we make our way up the front steps and informs us, "Mr. Johnson has company. He isn't accepting visitors."

"Either you hand us $50K, or we're going inside." Conor traverses the last couple of steps and squares up to the man, who towers over him.

The burly bloke laughs in his face. "I'd like to see you fucking try."

Conor shifts his gaze toward me, and I don't hesitate to take the last few steps. Swinging the bat as I reach the top step, it cracks against the burly bloke's kneecap with a stomach-turning crunch. As the guy crumples, Conor grabs the back of his shirt and tosses him to the side. Screaming in agony, he topples down the concrete stairs until he's sprawled on the sidewalk.

"You were saying?" Conor snarks as he pushes open the front door.

When I step inside behind him, I quickly count the number of men in the hallway. *Seven.* "Well, fuck," I mutter. "That's not an entourage. It's a personal fucking army."

Outnumbered, the three of us barrel into them with fists and bats flying. We manage to knock three of them to the ground before a meaty fist slams into my face. *Fuck, that's going to leave a bruise.* It hits with such force that it tips me off balance, and I slam into the wall in an attempt to catch myself. Furiously, I shove myself from the wall and lunge at the man who hit me, taking us both to the ground. He lets out an airy grunt when his back slams onto the hard marble floor of the foyer and knocks the wind out of him. Pinning him beneath me and straddling his chest, I pummel his face with a barrage of punches until he lies unconscious.

"That's for my fucking face," I snarl as I climb from his limp body. Declan hands me my bat as I get to my feet. The three of us head upstairs toward the grunts and moans of our mark and his *company*. Pushing our way into the bedroom, we find him balls deep in the ass of a petite brunette bouncing on his cock.

"What the fuck?" he spits as he continues to fuck her. "This isn't a fucking porn show. Get the fuck out."

"Nikki likes being watched," I retort, placing the face of the girl. "Isn't that right?"

"Long time no see, Finnigan," she coos, continuing to ride him without breaking her rhythm. She still looks good, except for her new fake tits. But they've clearly helped to level up the wallet-thickness of the men she's pulling these days.

Declan shoves my shoulder. "Are you fucking serious right now?"

"What?" I shrug. "She used to be my neighbor."

"Dudes," the bloke beneath her groans. "Get the fuck out."

"Time to go, Nik." I tip my head toward the door. "We've got some business with him that you don't want to see."

After casually slipping him from her ass, she climbs off him and then the bed. She struts toward the three of us, slowing when she reaches me. "Call me," she husks, dragging her finger over my chest as she walks past me naked. "You can finish what he clearly couldn't."

"You fucking whore," the erect bloke barks from the bed.

Shoving my bat into his chest, I growl, "We don't fucking talk to women like that. And trust me, your little guy definitely wasn't going to satisfy her."

"Does hot fucking pussy just fall in your lap?" Conor asks, pulling the naked man from the bed.

"Yeah. Pretty much," I answer before swinging the bat into the bloke's gut. He grunts, folding over in pain as Conor holds him upright for another swing. "For making us come all the way down here, we're going to beat the piss out of you. Whether or not you pay up, though, will determine if you can still walk tomorrow."

I swing the bat again, and Conor lets him fall into a naked heap on the floor. "The closet," he whimpers through the agonizing pain. "The safe is in the closet."

Holding him to the floor with the barrel of the bat, my eyes follow Declan retreating to the closet and returning a few minutes later with a couple of hefty stacks of cash.

"If you like getting the piss beat out of you, there are services for that." I kick my boot into his side, causing a gurgled cry to erupt from him. "They're a whole lot prettier than this lot and won't cost you $50K and a set of broken ribs, either." His eyes widen as I lift my boot, and he sucks in a deep breath in anticipation of my next move. *Rookie mistake.* Stomping down, his chest cracks beneath my boot, and a pained breath blows over his lips.

———

Having dropped both Declan and Conor at their places, I glance in the rearview mirror as I drive back to my place, getting my first look at the shiner growing beneath my left eye. My gaze falls back to the road, and I'm surprised to find a familiar blonde in athletic attire walking alone on the sidewalk.

What the fuck is she doing out by herself at this hour?

Her tight leggings and baggy athletic tank are a far cry from the very demure outfits she normally wears. Her curvy hips sway with each of her brisk steps, and I'm practically unable to pull my eyes from her ass.

She hasn't just garnered the attention of my wandering eye but also of the three men behind her. They aren't just following her. The three of them stalk closer with every few steps she takes. Their eyes roam over her with a nefarious hunger. They're hunting *my* prey.

How the fuck doesn't she realize they're following her?

CHAPTER TEN
CATLIN

Walking home from the gym, the hair on the back of my neck stands on end when the black SUV driving past me slows to a crawl. My heart begins racing, and I pick up my pace to a brisk walk.

"Hey," a slightly familiar voice calls from the window as it lowers. "Get in, Catlin. I'll give you a ride home. Or wherever it is you're going."

Finnigan?

"I...I'm good," I stammer, heeding Uncle Sean's warning. Even without it, I know better than to climb into cars with strange men. Especially in the middle of the night. "It's only a couple of blocks away."

He abruptly stops the SUV in the middle of the street and storms toward me on the sidewalk. I am completely fixated on his black eye and bloody lower lip; by the time my brain registers the idea of running, he's towering over me and reaching for my arm. As I recoil from him, he barks, "Get in the fucking truck, Catlin."

"I'd rather not." I vehemently shake my head.

"Trust me." He gestures behind me. "I have way better intentions than those three fecking blokes following you."

Suddenly spinning around, my heart leaps into my throat when I find three men not more than fifteen meters from me, hungrily eyeing me over. I might not know with certainty, but I can only imagine what their intentions were.

Or what would have happened if Finn didn't stop.

"Please." Finn softens his tone, outstretching his hand toward mine. "Get in the truck, Catlin."

With a heavy breath to gather my courage, I let him take my hand. Firmly holding it in his, he walks me toward the SUV still running in the middle of the street and opens the door for me to get in.

"What the hell are you doing walking out here alone this late at night?" he gruffly asks as he slides behind the wheel.

"I... um... I'm walking back home from the gym."

"And home is..."

"The church," I answer, and his brows furrow in confusion.

"Didn't anyone tell you it's not safe?" he presses as he slips the SUV into drive.

"Yes," I admit. "But it was only a few blocks."

"The same bad shit can happen in one that can in ten," he lectures.

Passing under a streetlight, the light illuminates the car enough that I notice the bloodied knuckles of his hand wrapped around the steering wheel. "From your appearance, I'm going to assume I'm not the first damsel-in-distress you rescued tonight."

"No, sweetheart." He chuckles. "These are from work. Not counting my favorite cute little redhead, you are the only pretty girl I've had in my car this week."

"Oh." The exclamation falls over my lips before I can stop it.

"Oh?" He coyly smiles. "Is that 'oh, the cute little redhead?' or 'oh, work?'"

"Both," I softly answer honestly.

"You've met the redhead. She's about three feet tall and absolutely adorable." I can't help but smile at his answer and how much he clearly adores his niece. "And I can only imagine Father O'Flaherty has told you plenty about what my family does for work."

I silently nod in agreement.

"It's true," he admits. "Whatever he may have told you, it's probably true."

Taking in his battered and bloody appearance as he admits that he's everything Uncle Sean said he is—a shameless womanizer, a thief, and a murderer—I don't feel the least bit unsafe sitting beside him.

"But... You saved me tonight..." My words trail off as I stare at him.

Pulling to a stop before the church, the leather of his seat crinkles as he turns to face me and replies, "Of course I did."

"It's just..."

"What? Tell me what you're thinking."

The streetlight above us causes his blue eyes to twinkle as he stares at me, awaiting my answer. My gaze wanders over his face and back to his eyes, which have a softness that I didn't notice when we first met. "Just... With what I've heard and how you talk to me... I can't help but wonder if you're a bad man who does good things or a good man who does bad things."

"I guess you'll just have to get to know me to find out." A flirtatious grin spreads across his face, causing heated crimson to creep over mine.

Uncle Sean would lose his mind if he caught me in this car. I don't know if it's the fact that I've never met a man like Finn or if it's how he looks at me, but there is definitely something keeping me from opening the door. Mustering every bit of courage I have, I blurt, "Okay."

That one word leads to hundreds more, and hours pass as we sit in his Bronco under the dim lighting and talk. Glancing at the dash, I realize it's a little after midnight. With a hesitancy due to being unsure of my own words, I mutter, "I should probably go."

With gravelly sureness, he responds, "I'd rather you didn't."

The warm flush he keeps causing spreads over my cheeks, and I struggle to maintain eye contact with him. "Thank you for the ride home."

"Any time," he croons as I reach for the door handle. Dusting his hand over my arm, he opens his door. "Let me."

Quickly slipping from the driver's seat, he rounds the SUV. He opens the door and extends a hand to help me from my seat. As I slide from the SUV, I am practically pressed against him when my feet hit the pavement. I breathe in his spicy vanilla-laced cologne as I stare up at him.

"I mean it." He delicately sweeps a strand of hair from my face. His fingers dust my skin as he tucks it behind my ear, and a surge of electricity pimples goosebumps up my body. He glides his hand over my bare shoulder and down my arm. He carefully pulls my phone from my grasp and swipes his thumb over it to find it locked. Gently cupping my hand, he presses my thumb to the censor to unlock it. He taps the screen, and a ding comes from his pocket as he lays the phone back in my palm. "Next time you need a ride this late at night, you have my number."

"Thank you." I lean into him and press onto my tippy toes to place a chaste, appreciative kiss on his cheek. When I accidentally meet his soft, warm lips instead, I gasp. Abruptly pulling back, my fingers replace his lips on mine, and I mutter, "I'm sorry."

"Don't be sorry, sweetheart." He drags his tongue along his lower lip. "That was the fucking highlight of my night."

My cheeks burn with embarrassment as I take a few steps backward. "Good night, Finnigan."

Not breaking our stare as he closes the passenger door, he coyly smiles at me and returns the sentiment. "Good night, Catlin."

CHAPTER ELEVEN
FINNIGAN

Fuck...

I look down at the uncomfortable bulge in my trousers and adjust myself.

The last time I got hard from a peck on the lips, I was probably about thirteen years old.

Watching the beautiful cause of my discomfort climb up the church steps, I walk around the Bronco to the driver's side door. I ensure she's safely inside before climbing behind the wheel and heading home.

My cock hasn't gotten the memo that Catlin and I went our separate ways about twenty minutes ago, and I'm still hard as a fucking rock when I walk through the door of my apartment. My phone dings, and I can't help but smile as I reach into my pocket, hoping it's her. Swiping it open, I sigh upon realizing it's definitely not the text I was hoping for.

NIKKI

I've been thinking about wrapping my lips around your cock since I got home.

I haven't stopped thinking about having a pair of soft pink lips wrapped around my cock, either. They just don't belong to Nikki. Not bothering to respond, I toss the phone onto the black granite of the kitchen counter. I walk past the dark-brown leather couch in the living room as I head toward my master suite. Undoing my pants as I walk, I push them low enough for my cock to spring free. I teasingly stroke myself as I pass through the threshold.

My fingers fumble in the dark to find the switch for the bedside lamp. Finding it and flipping it on, I grab the Fleshlight and lube from my nightstand. I kick off my shoes and climb onto the white duvet, settling against the gray tufted headboard. Squeezing a bit of lube into my palm, I slather it over my cock. I wipe the excess over my trousers and slip on the toy. Closing my eyes and teasingly rubbing it over my tip, my head lulls against the gray linen behind it, and I let out a deep, rumbling groan as she takes over my thoughts.

Sitting on her knees between my feet, Catlin's hands firmly rub up and down my thighs as her lips dust over the tip of my cock. She playfully teases me with wet kisses and light darts of her tongue, never actually taking me past her pouty pink lips.

She stares up at me with those innocent hazel eyes. I stare at the emerald flecks as her tongue swirls around my tip, and she sucks me into her mouth.

I inch the toy over my length, repeatedly sliding it over my tip, mirroring Catlin's mouth.

"Fuck, Cat," I breathlessly groan at my fantasy. "Your lips feel so fucking good. Can you take a little more for me?"

She grips the base of my shaft, fists it lightly and takes me deeper into her mouth. The flat of her tongue drags along the underside of my shaft as she fills her mouth with me, stopping before I reach her throat. Holding the back of her head, I lightly guide her over my length.

"Just like that," I exhale, sliding deeper into the toy with slow, languid strokes. "You're doing so fucking good sucking my cock."

My fingers entangle in her blonde locks, lightly guiding her as her head bobs between my thighs. Getting more comfortable, she picks up speed.

Gripping the toy firmly, I work it over my cock as moans continue to rattle from me. Fighting the urge to drag the toy over myself to the base, I groan, "I want to take your throat. Can you do that for me?"

Catlin stares up at me with trepidatious, wide eyes as she holds my cock in her mouth. Without pulling her lips from me, she nods lightly and mumbles, "Mmm-hmm."

"Such a good girl," I groan, sliding the toy over the entirety of my cock.

Fisting her hair, I push her over me, and she gags as I press into her throat.

It's a sad replacement for how good I imagine her mouth would feel, but I still need more. My hips rise to meet the silicone toy in my hand, and I fuck it hard and fast. Growls rattle from my lungs as I fight against my need to come.

Catlin slides me down her throat until her lips are pressed to the skin surrounding my base and I'm done for.

"Fuuuuck," I grit through my clenched teeth as my rigid cock twitches inside the toy. Ribbons of cum shoot from my tip until I've emptied myself into the silicone sheath.

Staring up at me, she eagerly swallows every drop. Her lips slide up the length of my shaft as she cleans any trace of my release from my skin. She licks her lower lip, gathering the bit of cum-tinged spittle hanging from it.

Climbing from the bed, I head into the adjoining bathroom. I turn on the shower and strip from the rest of my clothes, quickly cleaning the Fleshlight as I wait for the water to warm.

Finally stepping into the shower and standing under the warm spray of the water, I sigh. "I'm so fucked." Wanking to her did absolutely nothing to push her from my thoughts. Quite the opposite, actually; she's the only thing I can think about as I quickly clean up. I stay under the stream well after I'm done, but this feeling—this *need*—doesn't pass as the water runs cold.

After turning off the spray, I step from the shower. With icy droplets of water running down my body, I throw on a pair of sweats and pad into the kitchen where I left my phone. My thumb drags over the screen, and I swipe it open, revealing Nikki's text again. Without a second thought, I click on her name, delete her contact information, and pull up Catlin's as I head out the front door.

I can't stop thinking about your lips on me.

She doesn't need to know that it's my cock that I'm imagining them on the most.

CHAPTER TWELVE
CATLIN

My breath sputters as I read his message. I blink repeatedly, swearing that my eyes are deceiving me, before reading it again. But the words don't change. Holding the phone in my hand, I struggle to figure out how to respond. No one has ever texted me anything remotely close to that before.

And why would they?

Minutes pass with my thumbs resting against the screen, and another message from him pops up.

"No... I mean... I just don't know what to say," I record and send a voice message before I have the chance to overthink it.

> Fuck, I love how innocent you sound.

*That's because I **am** innocent.*

> How innocent are you?

> Have you never really been kissed before, Cat?

I can't type my response fast enough. I'm inexperienced, but I don't want him to think that my lack of experience goes *that* far.

> You weren't my first kiss.

> I might not have been the first lips you ever had on yours, but judging by your reaction, I'm pretty sure you've never really been kissed.

> Because I can't stop thinking about properly kissing you.

> Properly kissing me???

I nervously chew at my lower lip as I watch the dots, indicating he's typing his response.

> Pulling you tightly to me as my fingers tangle in your hair...

> Feeling your chest heave against me
> while you wait for me to press my lips
> to yours…

My breathing grows heavier with every incoming text, his words affecting me in ways I've never experienced.

> My warm breath blowing against your
> face as my lips dust over yours,
> causing your heart to flutter…

His texts come in slowly, only increasing my anticipation and leaving me hanging on his next words.

> That flutter traveling between your
> thighs as my tongue pushes between
> your lips and brushes over yours…

> Kissing you until you're completely
> breathless and my kiss is no longer
> enough.

I gulp so hard that I nearly choke.

That is absolutely nothing like the few times I kissed Andrew McIvner.

Andrew slobbered all over my chin and shoved his tongue down my throat with such carelessness it felt like I was being force-fed raw oysters. It doesn't even pale in comparison to what Finn is describing.

Reading his words, I remember how soft and warm his lips felt when I accidentally pressed against them.

Feathering my fingers along my lower lip, I imagine what it would feel like to have him truly kiss me the way he describes.

The phone buzzes as it rings in my hand, immediately pulling me from my thoughts. Swiping to answer, I stutter, "F...Finn?"

"I need to kiss you, Cat." His voice is filled with yearning desire. "Tell me you don't want me to and I'll leave."

"Leave? Are you... here?" My stomach flips, and my eyes dart to the door. Clamoring to my feet, I race to it and pull it open before he has a chance to answer. My jaw drops when Finnigan Evans is actually standing on the other side. Fisting his shirt, I pull him inside and shut the door as I huff, "You can't be here."

"Pulling me inside instead of sending me away is kind of sending mixed messages there, sweetheart," he teases as a smirk pulls at one corner of his mouth, causing a small dimple to mark his cheek.

"Uncle Sean will murder you and have my hide if he finds out you're here." His muscular arm snakes around my back, and I harshly whisper-shout, "I'm serious."

"So is my need to taste those lips of yours." He tightens the arm around my waist, and I crash against his hard body with a breathy grunt. "No one saw me."

Fueled by the nervous energy of getting caught and being this close to him, my heart races and my breathing grows incessantly fast. My nipples drag against his muscular body through my thin shirt with every rapid breath I draw.

"But if you tell me to leave, I will." His warm breath wafts over my face with every word that passes over his lips. Barely able to breathe, I look up to find his powder-blue eyes staring down at me.

Looking at me like that, I couldn't send him away if I tried.

"If you aren't telling me to leave, I'm getting what I came here for," he whispers, slowly lowering his face toward mine. I give a timid nod and shut my eyes as he closes what little distance there is between the two of us. His lips press against mine, and they're as warm and soft as they were a couple of hours ago.

This time isn't nearly as short, though. I kiss him back, loosening my lips slightly for the tender, wet—*definitely not Andrew-McIvner wet*—kisses being passed between us. His tongue darts from his mouth and licks teasingly against my lips, urging me to give him more. I give him what he wants—*what I want*—parting my lips, and his tongue presses into my mouth. He swirls it around, and I can taste the faint minty freshness when he massages it against my tongue.

His hands slide up my back as he continues to plunder my mouth. The rough drag of his hands over my shirt ignites a fire on the skin beneath it. Breathless and losing all resolve, I want more of him. *More, which I know I shouldn't.* Sliding my hands along his stomach and up his well-defined chest, I whimper into his mouth as I feel the muscular ridges hidden beneath his shirt.

The small mewl fuels him, and he kisses me headily. Finn moans into my mouth as his fingers drag the length of my spine, clawing at my skin so roughly it almost hurts. Splaying my hands across his chest, I use every ounce of my remaining willpower to push him from me and break our kiss.

"Fuck," he pants, stepping back from me. "You're going to ruin me, Cat."

Still breathless, I urge, "You should go."

Because you're already ruining me.

CHAPTER THIRTEEN
FINNIGAN

With my chest heaving as I stagger back from Catlin, the warmth of her lips on mine and her hands splayed across my chest still lingers. Her heavy words ring in my ears.

You should go.

Leaving is the last thing I want to do. The taste of her and the way she felt against me didn't just affect my—ridiculously hard again—cock. Kissing her was... *different.* I felt her *everywhere.* Her lips pressed to mine, and her body against my hands caused my stomach to flutter. The electricity between us tingled in my fingertips as they dragged along her skin. I want—*no, need*—to pull her back into me and kiss her until we're both completely lost in each other again. Until the need to claim every inch of one another is so unbearable that we're left with no choice but to give in to our desires.

"Cat," I exhale as I step toward her and outstretch my arm to drag her soft body against me again, but she shakes her head and shuns my reach. She lifts her stare from the floor, and the usual emerald sparkle of her gaze is gone, replaced with trepidation and a tinge of sadness.

Her breathing is ragged as she struggles to hold my stare. Her gaze falls to the floor again, and her pained voice crackles between her labored breaths, "I'm sorry."

Clouded with my arousal, I didn't see it at first. But it was written all over her face when she pushed away from me; what she felt was as terrifying as it was arousing. I could feel her need like it was my own —*because it **was** my own*. She needed more of me as much as her next breath. *If not more.* This thing between us is palpable and has an urgency that swells far beyond her innocence.

She's scared.

"Oh, Cat. You don't need to be sorry," I reassure her, watching as she tries to hold herself together for me.

My gaze wanders past her as I give her a moment to collect herself, and I take in her modest living arrangements. Spanning the room, I count the religious artifacts hanging on the walls and collecting dust on the shelves. One painting, two figurines, and four—no, five—crucifixes.

Fuck.

Closing my eyes, I let out a deep sigh and solemnly shake my head.

I'm such a fucking idiot.

"Quinn warned me... that you were a good girl... Fuck. I just didn't... didn't realize..." I mutter as I close the distance between the two of us. Slipping my finger under her chin, I tip her distressed face up to mine. "Fuck, Cat, if anyone should be sorry, it's me."

Tears well in her eyes as she holds my gaze, and her lower lip begins to tremble. "I can't do this... With you." Her words are so soft that they're barely a whisper.

"Tell me why," I gently demand, swiping my thumb over her flushed cheek to catch a rogue tear.

"I'm not that kind of girl, Finn." She lets out a heavy sigh.

"No, you aren't." Cupping her face in both hands, I stare down at her and confess, "As much as I want to kiss you and taste those sweet lips of yours for the rest of the night, you don't have to be that kind of girl for me."

Dipping my head, I place a soft, comforting kiss against her forehead.

"There have been... I've met a lot of women in my life, Cat, and you aren't like any of them." I continue to stroke my thumbs over her ruddy cheeks. "And I don't *want* you to be like any of them."

There's something different about her, and it isn't just her sweet innocence.

"You scare me, Finn."

"You don't need to be scared of me."

"I'm not afraid of *you*," she clarifies, shaking her head. "I barely know you. It's what I think about doing when you touch me that worries me."

"Then I won't touch you." Dusting my fingers along her jaw, I slide my hands from her face as I whisper, "Not until you ask me to."

Taking a few steps backward to place more distance between us, I find my back pressed to the door. I reach for the knob behind me and turn it to begrudgingly honor her request. I pull open the door and step over the threshold into the unseasonably brisk night air. Without breaking the gaze between us, I whisper, "However long you need."

A faint smile spreads across her face, and the emerald of her eyes regain a bit of their beautiful flicker when she softly purrs, "Good night, Finnigan."

"Good night, Cat." I hold her stare through the narrowing gap in the doorway until it clicks shut. Even once it's closed, and I'm standing exposed in the courtyard, I struggle to bring myself to leave.

Heading to the perimeter, I leave the same way I got in. I scale the brick wall and drop to the concrete sidewalk on the other side. Safe from the threat of being caught in the convent by Father O'Flaherty, I lean against the cool bricks and take a moment to collect my thoughts.

Did I really just promise to be abstinent for a woman I barely know?

"Fuck, Cat," I mutter to myself as I push myself from the brick wall behind me. "You really are going to fucking ruin me."

CHAPTER FOURTEEN

CATLIN

My thoughts are so scattered today that I can barely concentrate. Given that I spent most of the night staring at the ceiling; my current exhaustion isn't helping my scrambled brain.

Finn...

He has consumed my thoughts today. Finnigan Evans. His promise of however long it takes. That kiss.

Ugh... that kiss.

My lips tingle just thinking about letting him kiss me again. Thinking about it—and how badly I want him to do it again—kept me up most of the night. It's also what has had me so distracted that I've been drafting the same newsletter all afternoon.

A light knock on my office door startles me, but not

nearly as much as looking up to find Finn standing in the doorway. "What are you doing here?" I gasp.

"I came to confess my sins." He walks into the room and lowers his voice before continuing, "I couldn't stop myself from coming to see the reason behind them."

Members of the congregation don't come up here to the offices. But of all of them, Finn definitely shouldn't be up here. After spending all day thinking about him and wishing I could see him again, I can't bring myself to tell him that he needs to leave.

With his eyes locked on me, Finn rounds the desk, eases my chair from beneath it, and spins me slightly toward him. He places his hands on the arms of the chair, boxing me in.

Both loving and hating the effect he has over me, I softly whisper, "Finn..."

Hovering barely an inch above me, his warm breath blows over my lips and ignites the tingle I've been imagining all day. Swallowing hard, I hold his gaze as he confesses, "I said I wouldn't touch you, and I won't. But you need to know, Cat, it's the only fucking thing I've thought about doing since I left you last night. More than anything, I want to taste those lips of yours again."

Closing my eyes, my heart pounds as I grant myself the one thing I've desired all day. "Then do it."

With his weight braced on my chair, Finn dips his head and his lips dust against mine. He takes his time, kissing me gently and getting the taste he wants. Continuing to sample my lips, his fingers drag along my jaw before delicately circling my throat. I whimper against his touch when he ever so lightly tightens his grip. Smiling through our kiss, his words vibrate against my lips. "Not such a good girl after all."

I'm not...

The things running through my mind right now are absolutely sinful, yet I feel no remorse for them. I don't just want him to keep kissing me; I want to know what his lips and hands feel like all over my body.

What has he done to me?

As though he can read my mind, his hand slides down the length of my throat and over my shirt until he's cupping my breast. Tensing slightly at his touch, I don't push him away. I nod into our kiss, silently letting him know it's okay. My nipples grow hard as he kneads at my breast, and my chest heaves with every repeated squeeze. The electric tingle his palm gives to my nipple travels straight between my thighs. I squeeze them together in a futile effort to calm this foreign ache he's causing.

Pressing my palms against his chest, I lightly push him from me. He pulls his lips away without any hesitation. Still hovering just above me, he rubs his thumb along my jawline as he stands. As I not-so-innocently glance down his body, my eyes are drawn to the very large bulge at the front of his pants. "My thoughts aren't limited to merely kissing you." He adjusts himself.

Already flushed from our kiss, my cheeks grow hotter at his admission as I continue to stare at his tented crotch. There is a comfort in knowing I'm not the only one being tormented with need.

"I should go," he husks. "I can smell how fucking wet you are. With how sweet you smell, it's taking everything I have not to spread you across this desk and taste the rest of you."

"You want to taste me"—I glance down at my lap with a gulp and back up to his searing gaze—"there?"

Apparently, there was a lot omitted in the limited sexual education I have received.

With a devilish glint in his eyes, he gravelly whispers, "I don't *just* want to taste you, *piscín.* I want to feast on you until you're screaming my name as you come all over my tongue."

Staring up at him in silence, with my knees pressed tightly together, I'm clueless about how to respond to him. I blurt the first thing that comes to mind, "I've never done... anything."

"Anything?" He cocks an inquisitive brow.

"Anything," I repeat with embarrassment. Waiting has been instilled in me for a lifetime by my family and the church. It's what good little Catholics do. Yet, I'm pretty sure I'm the only good little Catholic girl on the planet.

"I always thought I'd wait until I was married. I've never met anyone that made me think about wanting to."

"Are you saying I make you want to be my naughty girl?"

My naughty girl?

"Your girl?" I clarify, trying to tame my excitement.

"Catlin O'Flaherty…" Leaning in, Finn slips his fingers under my chin and cups it. He places a soft, fluttering kiss against my lips. Staying a breath from me, his words vibrate across my lips. "You're going to be mine, Cat."

Sitting at a table in the club's lounge, I share a bottle of Jameson with my brothers. Well, Liam and Conor. Declan is stuck in traffic somewhere between his home in New Rochelle and here, and Tristan snuck off a while ago for an exhibitionistic fuck in one of the semi-private rooms with Layla.

Floral perfume floods my nostrils as a set of delicate feminine arms drape over me from behind. Loosely encircling my neck, a beautiful middle-aged brunette rounds my chair. The slit of her black silk dress parts as she takes a seat on my leg, revealing her well-toned thigh clear to where it creases at her hip. "It's Finnigan, right?"

"Finn," I correct her.

"Brooke. My husband, Carl, and I have watched you a few times from the hall. He's dying to watch me get fucked by a hot bull with a huge cock that will stretch me out. We both keep thinking that you'd be perfect. So, room six." She slips a key card into my shirt pocket, and her lips brush against the shell of my ear as a sultry voice whispers into it. "I love how hard you fuck. I'm hoping you mark me so much that he has to remember you ruining my pussy for him with every bruising bite I wear for the next week."

Fucking cucks...

"Right in your fucking lap," Conor mutters under his breath, his eyes roaming over the very eager and *very* forward woman draped across my lap.

Lightly holding her arm against my chest, I reach into the pocket of my shirt to retrieve the black-and-gold Triskelion card she slipped into it. "Sorry, sweetheart. You are beautiful, and I'm flattered, but I have other plans tonight," I decline the overt offer of destroying her pussy. Liam and Conor watch with inquisitive expressions as I slip the keycard back between her well-manicured fingers.

"I don't have other plans, Brooke," Conor chimes with a broad smile as I help her from my lap.

"Too bad you have a tiny cock," Liam jests, laughing as he playfully elbows him.

"Li, what the fuck?" Conor huffs as the woman saunters away from the three of us. Undoing his trousers to whip his cock out and prove the size of his manhood, he snarls, "A tiny fucking cock?"

Finally arriving and sitting at our table as Conor reaches into his trousers, Declan barks, "We've all seen your bejeweled anaconda, Conor. Keep it in your trousers."

Returning without Tristan and finding all the seats taken, Layla slips onto Conor's lap. "I'll vouch for you, big guy," she offers with a wink.

"Thank you." He slips his arm around her hip and pulls her up his thigh until she's firmly wedged against him.

"It's definitely at least adequate," she snarks.

Squeezing her tightly, he growls, "You're such a fucking brat."

"You fucking love it." She places a playful kiss on his cheek before grabbing his glass and taking a sip of whiskey.

*And Declan gives **me** shit about trying to fuck his wife.*

Rejoining the table, Tristan sets three ice-filled whiskey glasses on it. He grabs a chair from a nearby table and takes a seat, cocking a brow at Layla and Conor immediately beside him.

"Sorry, brother. She's my girl now," Conor teases with

a devilish smirk as he places a wet kiss against Layla's lips.

"You might want to know that"—he air quotes—"*your girl* had her lips firmly wrapped around my cock about five minutes ago." Tristan laughs as a disgusted grimace scrunches Conor's face.

"You know what happens when you're a little brat." Tristan drags Layla from Conor's lap and onto his own. Pulling her tightly against him and nipping her neck, he whispers what we all know is a warning of a correction to come in her ear. Turning his attention to the rest of us, he asks, "Besides my brother trying to steal my wife, what did I miss?"

"We are all just talking about Conor's tiny cock," I quip before throwing my head back and laughing.

"I'm not interested in Conor's tiny cock," Liam smirks. "I'm more interested in you. I have never seen you turn hot fucking pussy away. Especially when it's practically dripping on your lap."

"Wait? What?!" Tristan's eyes snap to me. "Finn did what?"

Refilling his glass, Liam responds, "You fucking heard me."

"A tall, brunette hot-wife, with perfect tits and an even better ass, basically begging to get thoroughly fucked and marked in front of her husband," Conor fills in the details. "And he passed because he had *other plans.*"

"It was much more polite than saying I wasn't interested." I shrug, trying to play it off. Looking around the table, no one is buying my bullshit. Least of all Declan, who is currently staring at me with furrowed brows and a clenched jaw.

"Spill it, Finn," Liam demands. "You're *always* fucking interested."

"Fuck." I eye Tristan and Declan. "Is this what it's like being on the receiving end of everyone needing to know what you are or aren't doing with your cock?"

"Yes," Dec snarls. "Now, fess up."

"It's not a big deal," I insist. "I told her I wouldn't until she was ready."

All of them asking the same question, the table choruses, "Her?"

"Will you ever fucking listen, Finnigan," Declan snarls. "How hard would it have been to stay away from Father O'Flaherty's niece?"

After last night? Fucking impossible.

"No sex?" Conor scoffs. "You won't make it one fucking week."

"Let me get this straight," Liam clarifies. "You're giving

up sex so that you can take that tight little blonde virgin for a ride?"

"Don't fucking talk about her like that." Shoving my chair from the table, my voice thunders over the patrons in the lounge, and the room momentarily goes silent. It takes a second for the crowd to return their conversations, but my family—with various looks of bewilderment—stares at my angered face in silence.

Yeah... I'm so fucked.

CHAPTER SIXTEEN
CATLIN

Rolling over in bed, I grab my phone off the nightstand as I stretch to wake up. The screen's brightness contrasts with the bedroom's darkness so much that it causes me to blink. It's a struggle to keep my eyes open to read the messages.

FINN

Happy Birthday, Cat.

Sorry if this wakes you, I wanted to be first.

I look closer at his message and realize he sent it a couple of hours ago.

You were definitely the first.

Good. I like the idea of being first with you.

I like the thought of it, too.

Sitting up to turn on the bedside lamp, I flip it on and am surprised to find a small powder-blue gift box with a white bow. Tentatively lifting it from the nightstand, I see the tag poking from beneath the ribbon.

To: Cat
From: Finn

Clicking the screen on my phone, I dial his number, and he answers on the first ring. "Good morn—"

"Did you seriously sneak in here last night, Finn?"

I should be absolutely terrified by the fact that a man snuck into my bedroom completely undetected while I slept, but I'm not. It's only been a few days, yet Finn has repeatedly shown me he respects my boundaries. *Well, mostly.* Breaking and entering—*or is it stalking*—is a pretty big boundary. But true to his word, he hasn't tried to so much as place a peck on my cheek since the other night.

"I told you, I like being first," he flirts. "Did you open it?"

"Not yet." I pull at the ribbon to release the bow so I can slide it from the box. Lifting the lid, I find a gold necklace with a small, delicate outline of a kitten dangling from the chain. The tone of my voice mirrors my smile when I confess, "It's beautiful, Finn."

"Not nearly as beautiful as you, *piscín.*"

How in the world does he keep causing me to blush with nothing more than a few words?

"Wear it tonight for me," he instructs. "I want to see it wrapped around that gorgeous neck of yours."

"I can't tonight. I have plans."

"I know," he confidently responds, and I suddenly feel he knows more about my plans with his sisters-in-law than I do. "I'll talk to you later. Enjoy your day."

"Finn," I call his name, hoping to catch him before he hangs up.

"Yeah, *piscín?*"

"Do not sneak in here when I'm sleeping."

"No promises because you're fucking beautiful when you sleep." I can almost hear the smirk spreading across his face as he hangs up.

———

FINN

I'm out front.

I will more than happily come inside to get you, but I don't want to fuck up your whole birthday by pissing off your uncle.

Shaking my head at his persistence, I reply to his message.

I told you I have plans.

You still do with Quinn, Layla, and Jorge.

They just changed a little, and I'm your ride.

Uncle Sean has some meetings with the diocese tonight, so he shouldn't be around. Even so, I'm not willing to risk Finn traipsing through the courtyard to the convent. The chance of getting caught is more than enough with him parked out front in one of those outlandishly large SUVs with tinted windows.

Grabbing my shoes, I head through the church and push open the heavy wooden door to see Finn leaning against a motorcycle. He's wearing dark denim jeans and a well-fitted black T-shirt that showcases his very defined physique. As I walk down the church stairs, he lifts a helmet from the back of the bike. Extending it toward me, he croons, "You look beauti—"

Interrupting him, I blurt, "Where is your car?"

"At this time of day, this is better for traffic." He taps his hand on the seat he's resting against.

"I'm wearing a dress. And... I'm not getting on that, Finn." I vehemently shake my head as my palms begin to sweat. Motorcycles have always made me nervous. Being on one, surrounded by the insane drivers filling the city streets, is absolutely terrifying.

"It's perfectly safe," he insists. "I promise I won't let anything happen to you."

I believe him. My heart thumps, and I swallow hard as I agree against my better judgment. "Okay..."

A broad smile spreads across his face as he steps away from the bike. He stares into my eyes as he reaches out his hand and tenderly tucks my hair behind my ears. My heart races faster, but it isn't nerves about the motorcycle anymore when he closes the distance between us. He gathers my hair into a loose ponytail at the nape of my neck and twists it down my back.

"It'll keep it out of your face," he informs me as he lifts the helmet over my head. It squeezes snugly and is much heavier than expected. The weight is only exemplified—and it pulls me off-balance—when he tips my head back to fasten the strap beneath my chin. Holding the strap, he pulls me toward him and kisses the helmet covering my lips. Even with inches of plastic and padding between us, my stomach flutters.

Finn puts on his helmet and climbs onto the bike before extending his hand to me. Holding onto him for balance, I hesitate for a moment before lifting my leg over the bike and climbing onto the seat behind him until I'm inches from his back. He pulls my hand around his body, and I instinctually wrap my other around him. Grabbing my wrists, he taps my hands against his abs and shouts through the helmet, "You hold on tight and lean when I do, understood?"

He turns over the ignition on the motorcycle, which vibrates beneath me. My arms tighten around him, squeezing so hard as I fist his shirt that it must hurt. "I've got you," he shouts over the rumble of the engine. Lifting the kickstand, he pulls slowly onto the street. We crawl with traffic for several blocks before coming to a stop at an intersection.

Finn reaches back with one hand and lightly taps my knee. His hand drags up the bare skin of my thigh to the hemline of my dress, tucked firmly underneath me, as he praises, "You're doing so good." Even with the hot summer air and the bike radiating heat beneath me, goosebumps prickle over my skin.

"Are you ready?" he asks, and I nod against him when my answer is muffled by my helmet. "Then, hold tight, *piscín.*"

He revs the engine, and the vibrations pleasingly rattle through my thighs and up my body. I squeeze my legs firmly against his to calm the tingling sensation as I grip his shirt harder. The light turns green, and I squeal as he peels through the intersection and onto the empty road before us. He continues to pick up speed, and I squeeze against him even harder. "Finn!" I nervously wince when we abruptly merge and whiz past a taxi. He weaves through the busy New York traffic with precision without slowing, and I watch as the city dwindles.

Where are we going?

With fewer cars on the road, Finn maneuvers the bike with only his right hand. He gives a gentle squeeze on my right hand to loosen my hold on the tight ball of cotton in my fist. As I tighten my left hand's grip, he pulls my right up to his chest and splays my fingers. His heart pounds against my palm just as hard as mine is against his back, and it takes a second for me to register that his is racing for a different reason. Lacing his fingers with mine, he holds my hand against him as we ride.

And suddenly, I don't care where we're going.

CHAPTER SEVENTEEN
FINNIGAN

Since promising to move at her speed a few nights ago, I have had only a handful of stolen kisses on church property with Catlin. *Not nearly as many as I would like.*

Choosing to use the Scrambler to drive her to New Rochelle is undeniably a cheap way to have her pressed against me, but I couldn't help myself. *I need more.* Had she refused the ride on my motorcycle, I would've had no issue using a rideshare instead.

But fuck, am I ever glad she didn't.

She clings to me so tightly, though, that I'm quite certain she needed this as much as I did. I relish in the feel of her arms wrapped around me and her thighs quivering lightly against mine with every mile. I've fucked my hand several times in the past few days, imagining her beneath me with her limbs wrapping around me just like this. Having her this close makes my cock twitch each time those images come barreling through my thoughts.

Fuck, Finn.

Pay attention to the road.

Slipping my fingers from hers, which are splayed across my chest, I rub her hand before retaking the handlebars with both hands to navigate a series of rapidly approaching sharp turns. Her arms tighten their hold—her hand remaining steadfast over my beating heart—as she effortlessly moves with me through every turn.

We pull to a stop before a tall, wrought-iron gate. I press the entry code into the call box on my left as Catlin taps my chest to garner my attention over the loud hum of the bike, shouting, "Where are we?"

"Your birthday dinner," I reply over the engine with a smirk beneath my helmet before pulling through the gate as it slowly opens and proceeding up the drive. Coming to a stop beside Tristan's Aston Martin, I lower the kickstand and turn off the bike before removing my helmet. I reluctantly slide Catlin's hands from me, and I tug lightly, gesturing for her to dismount. "You first, *piscín.*"

The moment she slides from behind me and climbs from the bike, I miss the feel of her against me. I watch for a second as she struggles to remove her helmet before lending her a hand. "Is this your place?" she asks as I place the helmet on the bike.

"No." I scoff. While I love this house and spend a ton of time here, I couldn't imagine a quiet life out here in the suburbs. "This is Declan and Quinn's place. Everyone is probably out back on the deck."

"Everyone?" Her voice ticks up. "I wasn—"

"Relax., *piscín*," I drape my arm around her shoulders and pull her into me. Pressing my lips to her forehead, I inform her, "It's just your friends and my brothers."

Like I've ever brought any girl to my family...

...but Catlin isn't any girl.

In an attempt to be a gentleman, I lead her around the side of the house with my hand pressed against the small of her back, Fiona announces our arrival. "*Uncail* Finn!" Running barefoot across the patio, dripping water from her swimsuit, she jumps into my arms when she reaches me.

"I hope you don't mind," Quinn apologizes as she joins us. "Finn was pretty insistent about moving your party here." She's under-exaggerating. I was adamant and wouldn't have taken no for an answer.

"I thought you said the plans had changed?" Cat looks up at me.

"They did—because I changed them." Tonight is the first night since that kiss that I knew she would be out from under the overly watchful eye of Father O'Flaherty, and I wasn't going to miss my opportunity to spend time alone with her. Carefully, I take her hand and intertwine my fingers with hers as my brothers approach us.

"*Cailín álainn*," Liam flirts as he reaches for her free hand.

Playfully shoving him aside, Conor takes her hand and marvels, "You are more gorgeous than Finn let on."

"I didn't think it was possible to be more of a flirt than Finn." Catlin nervously giggles as the two of them gush over her, and I suddenly understand Declan's displeasure over my harmless flirting with Quinn.

"Too beautiful, and definitely too sweet, to be with this arse," Tristan shares.

"*Pog mo thoin*." I grumble. Gesturing to each of them, I introduce Catlin to Conor, Liam, Tristan, and Declan.

"If he doesn't treat you right, let me know. I'll happily beat the piss out of him for you," Declan offers, taking her hand and formally introducing himself.

"Don't let him fool you," Quinn interjects, shaking her head at Declan. "These two will beat the piss out of each other because it's Tuesday."

"Based on the fact Finn is the only one of you with a black eye, I'm thinking he's usually the one to get the piss beat out of him," Catlin jests, and my brothers all erupt with laughter.

"Oh good," Liam snarks, slapping my arm and giving it a squeeze. "Another brat."

"Brat?" Catlin asks out of confusion. I have mentioned our club, but with her sexual inexperience, I haven't delved any deeper.

That time will come.

"I'll happily explain it to her if you haven't," Conor offers with a wink. "Demonstrations and all."

"Not a chance." I pull Catlin closer and whisper, "I'll explain, eventually. Let's start with dinner."

Knowing how quickly Catlin befriended Quinn—and subsequently Layla and Jorge—I expected her to fit in with my brothers. But watching her interact with them during dinner, she slots right in with my family better than I could have ever imagined. *Even with Declan, who has extensive reservations about our relationship.*

"Do we get to have cake now?" Fiona chimes as we all bullshit with one another over empty dinner plates.

CHAPTER EIGHTEEN
CATLIN

Finn's family, with cute little Fiona belting it the loudest, sings Happy Birthday to me as Quinn carries a cake to the table.

Surrounded by the Evans family—*half of whom were strangers no more than a couple of hours ago*—I can't help but think back on recent birthdays. Since losing *Mam* and *Daidi*, none of them have been like this. Every birthday passed like nearly any other day. Uncle Sean would ring me to bless my day, and *Máthair Dhríonna* would cook bangers and mash—because I still can't bring myself to tell her it's not my favorite meal. Until this moment, I didn't realize just how much I missed having a family.

Expletive-fueled insults and laughter fill the room, both growing more rambunctious with every pour of whiskey. These boys are crass and loud, but it is obvious how much they all absolutely love one another.

Fighting back tears and falling apart at the table, I stare down at the flickering candles. They adorn a remarkably gorgeous cake frosted entirely in powder-pink roses and pearls. Finn rubs his hand over my back, bringing me back from my solemn thoughts. "Make a wish, *piscín*."

After taking a deep breath, I blow it over the cake and extinguish each of the candles as I make my wish.

A family as lovingly dysfunctional as this one.

We finish dessert, with the Evans family treating me as one of their own. I try to help clean up but am quickly shooed out of the kitchen. "Guests don't clean up," Declan declares. "Especially when it's their birthday."

Leaving the kitchen before I'm scolded again, I wander out to the patio and stare over the rail to the ocean beyond. Small waves lap at the shore as the moonlight flickers over the dark water beneath it. It's so mesmerizing that I don't hear Finn approaching until his arms wrap around me from behind. His lips press into the crook of my neck, and my body melts into his.

"Come." The lone word vibrates against my skin as he slips his hand into mine. With our fingers enlaced, he leads me from the patio and down to the beach. Slipping off my sandals when we step onto the beach, I toss them toward the patio steps. The sand squishes between my toes as we stroll along the shoreline to a more secluded area hidden by some rocks and out of his family's sight.

This is the first time I have truly been alone with Finn since we met. Sitting on the sand next to him, my nerves cause my heart to beat a little faster, knowing that no one is watching us and there is no chance of getting caught with him. No reason not to do the sinful things I've been thinking about.

Except for that promise to God.

"Did you have fun tonight?" Finn asks as his knuckles drag along my jaw and his soft-blue eyes bore into mine.

"Yes. So much. Your family is just... They're incredible."

"They all adore you," he shares. Hooking his arms around me, Finn pulls me into his lap. My heart thumps faster with every racing beat as I straddle his thighs with his hands resting on my hips. Slowly leaning forward, he pauses a breath from my lips and whispers, "*I* fucking adore you."

His lips press against mine, and I melt into their soft warmth. With my arms wrapped around Finn's neck, his hands trail up and down my spine. He presses his tongue between my lips and massages against mine. Effortlessly, Finn drags me up his thighs, and I whimper into his mouth as he holds me tightly to him.

Our chests heave in unison as we steal breaths between our needy kisses.

Finn's hand rests on my bare thigh, dusting over my skin at the hemline of my dress. Inch by inch—as though he's waiting for me to stop him—he works under the loose skirt until his fingertips are running along the edge of my panties. Shifting my weight, I brush against his growing length beneath me. I gasp at both the sensation of him and knowing that he's hard.

"Do you like the feel of me against your pussy?" Finn grips my ass with both hands and pulls me flush against his hips as he flexes. The hardness in his pants rubs against my panties, and a whimpered moan spews from me at the pleasurable tingle. My hips grind against him, wanting more. *Needing more.* Firmly holding my ass, he helps me ride his gyrating hips.

My head falls back, relishing in the pleasure swelling at my core. Finn's lips are immediately on my neck, traveling the length of it with his teeth and tongue. "Finn," I breathlessly exhale his name, the growing ache becoming unbearable.

"Is my good little *piscín* going to let go? Are you going to soak those little cotton panties from rubbing against my cock?" he groans against my neck between wet kisses and teasing bites.

I shouldn't.

We should stop.

But my body disagrees. Clawing at Finn's shoulders, I need more. As though he can read my mind, Finn pulls me tight and lays me in the sand as he climbs on top of me. Hovering above me, his large, tattooed hand slides up my thigh until the skirt of my dress is bunched around my waist. He looks down at my body and groans, "I love how fucking wet you get for me. Those little pink panties of yours are soaked."

His hand slides over my hip and his fingers dip beneath the waist of my panties, but I tense beneath him. He quickly withdraws his hand and places it back on my thigh. "We won't do anything you don't want. I'll stop the second you say so. I told you, as long as it takes."

"No." I lightly shake my head and stammer through my confession, "It's not that. Just... I've never. Not just with a guy. But... never."

His eyes don't leave mine as he whispers, "Until now."

CHAPTER NINETEEN
CATLIN

Lifting my hand to his face, Finn kisses my palm. He draws my middle and ring fingers into his mouth and lightly sucks and swirls his tongue over them. They are covered in his saliva when he pulls them out of his mouth. He shifts his weight to lie beside me and drags my hand between my thighs. Placing a soft kiss just below my ear, he slides both our hands beneath the waistline of my panties. "We're going to learn what you like together."

With our hands touching me, Finn rubs my fingers through the small tuft of hair and toward the source of my aching. He presses my fingers through my slit and slides them along the silky wet skin as my hips lift to meet our hands. Finn leads me, so I slide my fingers higher, and my breath sputters when we brush along my clit. He glides my fingers in light circles around the sensitive spot, and I whimper with need, "Finn. Please."

"Show me how badly you want me to make you come." He rubs my fingers over my clit, and the pleasure swells in my core so quickly I feel like I'm going to explode. My chest heaves with every brush, each breath becoming faster and more desperate. "You look so beautiful playing with your pussy. Keep going. Bring yourself right to the edge."

I follow his command and tease my clit, even as he slides his hand from mine. The rough sand scratches against my shoulders as my back arches from the ground and I lift my hips, sliding my fingers through my arousal and over my clit. "I just want to see all of you." Gripping my panties with two hands, Finn pulls lightly before asking, "Can I?"

Lifting my hips, I silently grant him the permission he needs. The damp cotton slides along my skin as he removes my panties from covering my pussy. When he's pulled them down my legs, he brings them to his face and draws a deep breath that causes a feral groan to rattle from him. "You smell like fucking heaven. *My* fucking heaven," he groans before tucking them into his jeans pocket.

I pant, and my lower lip quivers as he places his hand over mine again and slides it toward the source of my wetness. He rubs my fingertips through my arousal, teasingly pressing them into me. Gripping my middle finger, he slides it into me to the knuckle as I groan his name.

"No, *piscín*. That's all you." He smirks. Holding my hand and slowly sliding the digit in and out of me. "I don't want to hurt you. We need to warm up that tight little virgin pussy with your little fingers before I slip one of my thick ones in."

Peppering soft kisses over my neck, Finn continues to pleasure me with my finger. Struggling through every labored breath, he works me until every nerve in my body tingles on the edge.

"You're doing so fucking good for me," Finn praises as he kisses my forehead. "Can you take a little more?"

Unable to speak and ready to explode, I chew at my lower lip and nod.

"Good girl," he croons, pressing against my already occupied pussy. He pushes his fingertip into me. The welcome intrusion burns a little as it stretches me, and a broken whimper falls over my lips as he slides it slowly along the length of my finger until they're both fully seated inside me. My thighs tremble as he lightly thrusts our fingers in and out of me.

"Fuck, I could come just thinking about being inside this tight little hole," he groans as I quiver around us. I claw at Finn's shirt as the pleasure building at my core becomes nearly unbearable.

This feels too good to be wrong...

Finn presses another finger into me and curls them. All three of our fingers drag along my walls, and the ball of energy at my center explodes. A cracked scream rattles from my chest as the wave of pleasure shatters me, my back arching from the ground and my toes dig into the sand as I come.

Finn gingerly pulls our fingers from inside me, and I squeeze my thighs together to quell both the tender pleasure still vibrating inside me and my sudden shame. Grabbing my dress, I pull it down my thighs to cover myself and mutter, "We shouldn't have done that. I should've told you to stop—"

"*Piscín*, if you didn't want to—"

"I *did* want to," I exclaim. "That's the problem. It was wrong, yet all I can think about is doing it again."

"There is nothing wrong about what we just did. Or the things either of us are thinking about doing."

"You know that's not true, Finn." I huff. "I'm a good Catholic girl."

"You're still a good Catholic girl," he insists.

"You know that's not true." I lecture, "It's a sin... Giving into lust. Good Catholic girls don't sin."

He doesn't say a word as he grabs my hand and pulls it toward his mouth. With his eyes locked on mine, he places our fingers—which were all just inside me—into his mouth. Moaning around them, he diligently sucks and licks them until they are clean of me before pulling them out. "Sins don't taste as fucking good as you." He peppers the words against my fingertip and down to my palm.

I love and hate how Finn makes me feel. The things I do with him and the way he makes me question absolutely everything I know about my faith. Every doubt I have about whatever this is and what we just did disappears the second he presses his lips against mine. With the delicate feather of his lips and the tender sweeps of his tongue, he claims my mouth.

He claims me.

His lips hover against mine as he whispers, "If this is a sin, then hell will be my heaven. *You* will be my heaven, because I would happily fucking burn for you."

CHAPTER TWENTY

FINNIGAN

"Did you kids have a nice walk on the beach?" Conor jokes with a huge smile as we head back up the patio steps to find him sitting at the fire pit with Jorge and Layla. "Good *stargazing* on the beach?"

"Oh, someone *definitely* saw stars," Jorge razzes. "Pretty sure they heard her coming way out in Montauk."

"Jesus Christ, Jorge." Layla smacks his arm as Cat's face turns a hot shade of red that I don't think I've ever witnessed before.

"What?" Jorge shouts, rubbing his arm. "I'm jealous. Do you know how long it's been since I was fucked so good I screamed like that?"

"I am not above beating the piss out of you too, Jorge," I threaten. Catlin is struggling enough with our rela- tionship, she doesn't need these assholes getting into her head about it too. "You might not be one of my brothers, but you are family. And that makes you fair game." Jorge quickly throws his hands up in surrender as I playfully stalk toward him.

It takes us nearly an hour to say thank you and goodbye to everyone, which gets us back to the church significantly later than either of us had planned. Driving past the entrance, I assume Cat also notices that the church van is back already when she squeezes me tightly. I turn down the block that runs along the brick wall I've used to sneak onto the property a few times. Sending her over the wall sans panties isn't exactly how I planned to get her home tonight.

Gripping her waist, I hoist her so she can climb onto the wall. As she sits on the ledge, I vault over to help her down the other side. Hidden from view by the convent, I press her back to the brick wall and cage her against it. Claiming her mouth again, I kiss her until we're both breathless before pulling back. "I should go."

"You should," She palms my face and pulls me back in for another passionate kiss.

After pushing away from her, I slam my back against the brick of the convent. My eyes hungrily roam over her body as I adjust myself. "I have to go, *piscín*. I don't trust myself to stay."

"I don't trust myself to let you," she exhales. "Go."

With a single leap, I make it onto the top of the wall before dropping down to the sidewalk below. I wait until I hear her shut the door before climbing back onto my bike. During the entire ride home, the only thing I can think about is sinking inside of her. My whirlwind of fantasies is so fucking vivid that I'm hard as a fucking rock when I park my bike in the garage.

It's going to take one hell of a cold shower to tame this.

I head toward the bathroom to shower when I get home. Shoving my hand into my pocket, I am pleasantly surprised that I still have Catlin's panties. I pull them out and roll them in my hand. groaning when I realize they are still damp. Lifting them to my face, I take a deep breath and inhale her delicious scent as I strip from my clothes.

Fuck, does she ever smell good!

My phone buzzes, and I pull it from my pocket to find two texts from Catlin. She must've texted while I was riding home.

CATLIN

Was I really that loud?

And do you have my panties?

A broad smile spreads across my face as I breathe her scent in again before texting her back.

> I'm already preparing to soundproof my apartment

> And yes, I do.

> They smell like your sweet heaven.

The phone rings, and I quickly answer it. "Yes, *piscín?*"

"Are you seriously at home sniffing my panties?" Her voice ticks up with disbelief.

Fuck the cold shower...

"I am, and I'm so fucking hard thinking about you." I suck in a deep breath as I rub my hand along my shaft.

"Oh..."

Putting the phone on speaker, I drop it onto the counter. "You can hang up, or you can listen to what you do to me. The choice is yours, *piscín.*"

I wrap my hand around my cock and slide it along my length. It is a sad substitute for the tight warmth I want to be inside. Moans rattle from me as I fist my shaft.

"Are you thinking about me?" Cat's timid voice comes through the speaker.

"You're the *only* fucking thing I think about," I groan. "Every night, I fuck my hand thinking about how much I want to be inside you."

The phone is silent, but Cat hasn't hung up. My good girl is curious. There is a naughty side of her just dying to get out.

"I can't stop thinking about you coming around my fingers," I pant as I fist myself faster. "How fucking tight you were... And fuck... How fucking hard you came around me."

"I liked..."

"Don't be shy, *piscín*. Be a good girl and tell me what you like as you listen to me stroke my cock. Make me come all over your panties."

"I liked how you felt inside me," she softly responds.

"You'll fucking love how I stretch and fill you when you're ready to take every inch of my cock."

"Y...yes...," she stammers before confessing, "I've been thinking about that since you left."

"Fuck..." I exhale. Fighting against my release, my groans echo off the walls of the master bathroom. But listening to her talk about wanting me inside of her, I lose all control. Guttural moans rattle from my chest as I shoot ropes of cum into the damp panties I've been sliding along my shaft.

With her cum-filled panties in my fist, I slump over the counter. I struggle to catch my breath and realize that she, too, is panting. "Did your panties get wet listening to me come?"

"You have my panties, Finnigan."

"If you only have one pair," I tease, "I guess I'll have to return them to you in the morning. See you soon, Catlin."

"Good night, Finn."

"Good night, birthday girl."

CHAPTER TWENTY-ONE

CATLIN

Sitting on the sidewalk, Finn and I rest our backs against the brick wall surrounding the courtyard. This meager slab of cracked concrete has been our date spot for the past week. He's met me here every night to sit and talk.

Having my cum-stained panties returned to me the morning after my birthday party made me realize that this was all going way too fast. This *very* public location was meant to slow down the pace at which our relationship was progressing, but it has totally backfired on me. This sidewalk has proven to be a more intimate location than the beach—just emotionally instead of physically.

Instead of slowing down, I'm falling head over heels for him.

"I have to get going," Finn informs me after glancing at his watch. "We have an event at the club tonight, and I promised Tris I would be there to help. I'll text you in a couple of hours when I get home."

"Take me," I blurt my demand, ready to climb onto his bike.

"The club isn't a place for good girls like you." He shakes his head and places a soft kiss against my forehead, unwilling to entertain my request.

"Finn," I plead, pressing my hands to his chest and staring up at him.

"Please. Go inside and get some sleep, *piscín*. We can talk about this tomorrow," Finn urges, not giving me much choice as he helps me up and onto the wall.

If he won't take me, I'll just go on my own.

Swiping open my phone, I order an Uber before the roar of his bike has even gotten out of earshot. *Five minutes.* After running inside, I quickly change from my jean shorts and tank top into a white sundress Finn bought me a few days ago. The Uber is arriving when I walk out front, and I quickly climb in to catch up with Finn.

"Most people go to church after they've been here. Not before," the driver quips as he pulls to a stop before the club. "Considering you went first, enjoy your night, honey."

Ignoring his comment, I slide from the car and walk toward the velvet ropes and bouncer at the front door. He eyes me over, grunting, "Card?"

"I... uh... I don't have one," I stammer. "I'm here to see Finnigan Evans."

The tall, muscular bouncer's eyes scan over me once again, and he lets out a dark chuckle. "Sure, sweetie."

"Cat?" Jorge's voice tics up an octave when he passes me. "Does Finn know you're here?"

"No," I answer. My gaze darts to the bouncer, ensuring he heard Jorge. "*He* won't let me in."

"She's with me," Jorge tells the bouncer as he flashes his card.

The bouncer shakes his head, still denying my entry. "You know I can't, Jorge."

"She's Finn's girlfriend," Jorge presses. "I vouch for her, and you know he'll be fucking pissed to find out you made her wait out here. You know what he's like."

Hesitantly, the bouncer lifts the velvet rope to allow me through, and I take Jorge's arm to walk inside. We walk through a sleek lounge filled with well-dressed people enjoying a few drinks. Scanning the room urgently, my heart picks up pace. "I don't see him, Jorge."

"He's probably in the back of the club," Jorge suggests as we continue down a long, dark hallway. It's dimly lit, with only a few gold sconces illuminating the space.

Upon reaching the end, my feet root in place at the sight before me. It's like the small lounge we passed through, but so very different. Everything is black, and the people here aren't wearing the same expensive suits and dresses. Back here, most of the women are proudly parading around in lingerie.

"Wait here," Jorge instructs, noting my discomfort. "I'll go find him for you."

"No." I take a deep breath and step into the room. Curiosity has taken hold, and I want to see. I need to know what Finn does here. Slipping my arm from Jorge's, I mutter, "I'm fine. Go to work. I'll find him."

"Are you sure?" he asks, and I nod.

Walking through the room, I can feel the sets of eyes raking over me. As I continue to look for Finn, I catch a glimpse at a few of the faces; they range from inquisitive to carnal. A tall, bearded man approaches me with a heated gaze. My skin crawls as he steps close and runs a hand down my bare arm, flirtatiously asking, "Are you lost, darling?"

"I'm looking for Finnigan Evans," I answer, and the man takes a quick step away from me as though he's suddenly terrified to be seen with me.

"Sorry," he asserts. "I didn't realize... Back hallway." He gestures toward a corridor on the opposite side of the room. Walking toward it, I watch couples disappear into its depths. I reach the entrance before pausing for a moment and swallowing hard. *You've come this far.*

Couples line the narrow hall, some nuzzled together, staring through large windows into rooms on the other side. A gasp flies from me when I pass the first and find a woman tied to a bench as a man has sex with her. Passing two more windows, I see things I could have never imagined. Things well beyond the physical relationship I have had with Finn so far.

Is that why he comes here?

Passing another window, I pause briefly when I recognize one face on the other side. *Conor.* He's savagely thrusting into a woman I've never seen from behind as she takes another man in her mouth. Heat flushes over my face, watching their intimate act.

Is that what Finn left me for?

Intrusive thoughts take over as I continue to pass more windows, watching their intimate acts for a few seconds. Relief washes over me that the faces I'm seeing on the other side of the glass aren't Finn's.

Light spills into the hallway when a door opens a few rooms from me. Glancing into the illuminated section of the hallway, my heart breaks in two. Finn is standing beside a beautiful brunette in a sleek black dress and ridiculously tall matching heels. He's holding the door and places his hand on the small of her bare back, tenderly ushering her into the room.

It is what he left me for.

Trembling in place, pained tears roll down my cheeks as I struggle to find the strength to turn and leave. Finn glances down the hall, and his eyes widen when they land on me, his skin paling to a ghostly white.

CHAPTER TWENTY-TWO
FINNIGAN

"Really?" Jillian scoffs when I tell her what I want.

"Is it that hard to believe?"

"Finn, I've been listening to wild stories about the trashy women you date for years. Not once have you ever asked me to put any of them on your body," she retorts as we make our way down the hall.

We've set up two exhibition rooms for couples tattoos this evening. Having entrusted Jillian with nearly every drop of ink on my body, it was only fitting that we invited her to be one of our exclusive artists tonight. She's booked solid for the night, but has graciously agreed to add a little ink to my chest piece before leaving. Apparently, she's actually looking forward to taking a little creative freedom after the schedule of *good girl* and *Daddy* tattoos she has ahead of her tonight.

"She's not like them," I inform her. "She's sweet and innocent. Everything I didn't know I wanted."

Raising a brow, she teases, "Clearly. I never thought I'd see the day a woman managed to tame the great Finnigan Evans. She must have a magical fucking pussy."

"I wouldn't know."

"Hold up, you've been seeing this woman for weeks, you're putting her on your body, **and** you haven't fucked her!" she exclaims. "Fucking hell, Finnigan Evans is in love."

Opening the door, I place my hand on the small of her back, leading her into her studio. When I look down the hall to check the event is going as planned, I'm shocked to find Catlin staring back at me. Wearing the white sundress I bought her, she stands out like a sore thumb among this crowd. *But as gorgeous as she is, she stands out in any crowd.* She swipes at her face, and I realize that she's crying.

Breaking eye contact with her for a second, I peer into the room at Jillian and suddenly realize how this must look. "Fuck," I exhale, turning back to Cat, but it's too late. She isn't waiting for an explanation.

And I don't fucking blame her.

"Cat!" I shout after her as she shoves through the couples lining the hall, racing from me. Loud grumbles and my yelling create a scene and draw a larger audience. Fighting my way through them and pushing people out of my way, I continue to call after her, "Catlin! *Piscín!*"

She doesn't stop. Rushing down the hallway toward the lounge, she barrels through the exit and into the city. Horns blare from outside the club as she darts across the busy street. I throw open the door, and my heart stops when a cab narrowly misses her. "Catlin!" I shout, waiting for a small break in traffic as she puts more distance between us.

The break doesn't come, and I step into oncoming traffic to follow her. *I can't lose her.* I sprint down the sidewalk and into Bryant Park after her. Eventually closing the distance between us, I reach for her. "Stop, Catlin. Please. It's not what you think."

"That's what everyone says," she cries through sobs. "Just leave me alone."

"I can't." I huff, lunging at her. Crashing into her harder than intended, I roughly take us both to the ground. She screams, and her limbs flail as I pin her beneath me. Angrily shoving her wrists into the ground beside her head, I snarl, "Stop and fucking listen."

Tears stream down her face, painting it with trails of mascara, as she continues to fight me. "Let me up!" she shouts through her anguish.

"Nothing happened at the club." I stare down at her, keeping her pressed to the cool grass with my weight. "Nothing happened or was going to happen with Jillian. She's a friend and not one I've fucked or want to fuck. I don't want any of the women at the club. I only want you." My tone is harsh, but I need her to understand.

"Let. Me. Go!" she yells, still fighting against my tight hold, not registering what I'm saying to her.

"Don't you hear me? I can't," I breathlessly confess, sliding her hands through the grass above her head. "I can't let you go, Cat. I'm never going to let you go."

She stills beneath me, and the moonlight reflects off the soft green in her pained hazel eyes, rogue tears still falling from them.

If I never see her hurt like this again, it'll be a lifetime too soon.

"You're it for me, *piscín*," I whisper before placing a soft kiss against her lips and releasing her hands. "You can leave, but I won't be able to let you go," I confess, rolling off her.

"Finn..." My name cracks over her lips as we both stare up at the stars. "Do you love me?"

More than I have words to describe.

"Your name is carved across my heart." I roll to face

her and wipe the tears from her cheeks. "Do you love me, *piscín?*"

She closes her eyes, and her throat bobs as she takes a hard swallow before she gives a gentle nod. Cupping her tear-stained face, I pull her toward me and softly kiss her salty lips.

Helping her from the ground, I notice the grass stains on the back of her dress and that the strap tore when I tackled her. "Let me take you home."

"The club? Don't you need to go back?"

"No. I can't bring you back there like this." I fix her dress to ensure it's covering her. "They'll be fine without me while I take you home."

Flagging down a taxi, we ride in silence with her nuzzled against me. As much as I want to take her back to my place and spend the night apologizing to her and professing my love, I know this is what she wants.

CHAPTER TWENTY-THREE
CATLIN

After saying good night to Finn, climbing out of the cab and walking up the church steps isn't right. Walking away from him feels wrong.

When I sneak into the convent, I'm taken aback by my appearance in the mirror. My hair is a disheveled mess, and trails of mascara are smeared across my cheeks. I strip from my ruined dress, and I hop into the shower to clean the makeup and grass stains from me.

I put on a pair of cotton shorts and a white tank top before brushing the knots from my tangled hair. My reflection smiles back at me when my thoughts drift to Finn.

He loves me.

In the short time I've known Finn, he's changed so much. Or maybe it's just my perception of him that has. I've changed, too. He makes me question things I have blindly accepted my entire life. There's a whole world that I've been denying myself; one that he is so eager to show me.

Why the hell am I sitting here?

Before the thought has left my head, I grab a hoodie from the closet and toss it over my tank top. Next, I throw on a pair of Converse and head out the door. Quickly scaling the wall around the courtyard, I slide down the bricks, which are slick from the light mist. Pulling the hood of my sweatshirt over my head, I shove my hands into my pockets and begin walking.

Two blocks from his apartment, the sky booms with thunder, and the light mist becomes a heavy down-pour. Suddenly soaked to the core, I feel as though God is trying to give me a sign; I start second-guessing my decision.

You've come this far, Cat.

When I reach Finn's building, I'm surprised at how quickly the doorman lets me in. I've only been here once, and it was only for a matter of minutes so Finn could grab something from his apartment.

My shoes squeak across the white marble tiles in the lobby as I make my way to the elevator. When the cab arrives, I step in and push the button for the top floor, trying to remember Finn's apartment number. The elevator dings when I reach the eighteenth floor, and I hesitate so long to exit that the doors begin to close.

Shoving my hand into the small gap, they push back open for me to step into the hall. Walking fast and fueled entirely with nervous energy, I make my way to his door and read the number, confirming it's the right one.

What are you doing?

Water from my soaked hair trickles down my face, and my sodden clothes are dripping into a puddle around my feet. My fist thumps against his door, the rapping of my knuckles as fast and loud as the pounding of my heart. It's nearly 2:00 a.m., and I'm going to rouse his neighbors, but I don't care. This can't wait, because I'm already beginning to lose my nerve as I wait for him to answer.

"I'm tired of pretending," I blurt when Finn opens the door. He stares at me with wide eyes, no doubt questioning why I'm soaked *and* on his doorstep. Stepping into the open threshold and looking up at him, I take a deep breath and exhale, "I don't want to be a good girl."

"Cat?" He gazes at me in disbelief that I'm on his doorstep. "You're soaked. Did you walk here in the rain?"

"Yes," I mutter as he pulls me into the apartment and shuts the door. Water drips from me onto his hard-wood floor, but I can't pull my eyes off him. He's wearing nothing but black boxer briefs, leaving nearly all of him on display. The geometric ink covering his neck and arms covers every inch of his torso. My eyes roam down his pronounced pecs and over his rippled abs to the large bulge beneath the tight cotton of his boxers.

He's hard.

"I told you; every night." He smirks at my overt stare. "What are you doing here?"

Unable to think straight, I repeat, "I don't want to be a good girl."

Finn takes a step toward me and puts his fingers under my chin. Angling my face up to him, he shakes his head. "You don't have to do that for me."

"It's not for you," I correct him. "It's for me."

"Are you sure?" he presses, keeping the distance between us.

My heart pounds against my rib cage as I stare into his blue eyes. His concern and the adoring look in his eyes solidify my decision. I'm nervous as hell, but I have never been more sure of a decision in my entire life.

Placing my hands on his firm, bare chest, I step into him. He stands unwaveringly still, waiting for my response. I keep my eyes locked on his, and I pull my hands from him before slowly lowering the zipper of my hoodie. Slipping it from my shoulders, the heavy, drenched cotton plops to the floor.

"Cat." Finn's eyes trail down my body. My white tank top is soaked through, leaving my braless breasts on full display beneath the now sheer fabric. The adoring look in his eyes grows ravenous with every second. Finn's hand slides along my hip and up my side, and my breath hitches when his fingers dust along the side of my heaving breast. My fingers dance over his chest as he traces along the cup of mine.

"Please," I beg, wanting more of his touch. Needing to feel him on me. Wanting to experience everything that he wants to share with me. "I want to burn with you, Finn. Show me what your heaven is like."

Catlin, standing before me, soaked and begging for my cock, checks so many boxes of my fantasies that I struggle to believe this moment is really happening.

Her already tight nipples grow harder with every caress of my hand along the teardrop of her pert tits, pushing them against the sheer wet fabric of her tank top. She squirms when I slide my fingers along her sides and they dust her flank, and I note that my girl is ticklish. Gripping the hemline, I insist, "We should get you out of these wet clothes, *piscín*."

She nods timidly, lifting her arms as I pull the clinging cotton from her. After removing it from her entirely, I toss it haphazardly to the floor, causing droplets of water to splatter over both our legs when it hits the hardwood.

"You are so fucking gorgeous." I draw out every word of my exclamation as my eyes roam over her body. As I dip my fingers under the waistline of her shorts, I run them along her skin, prolonging the moment that I finally get to see all of her. The sodden shorts drop down her legs after I inch them over her hips, and they pool over her sneakers. She lifts each of her feet, stripping from the shorts and kicking off her sneakers, leaving her completely bare before me. "So fucking perfect," I groan, raking over every inch of her.

Pulling her close, a low grumble rattles from me when her nipples dust against my bare skin. I dip my head to her, and I press my lips to hers, feeling them trembling against mine. Pulling back and slipping my hand under her chin to keep her gaze up at me, I remind her, "You can tell me to stop at any time."

"No. It's just... I've heard..." Her voice trails off, and she lowers her gaze to my thick, cotton-covered cock currently wedged between us.

"It doesn't have to hurt," I reassure her, running my fingers along her spine. "The last thing I want to do is hurt you, Catlin."

"Okay," she mutters as she nods. Her rigid body relaxes slightly, my words helping to ease her anxiety.

"You'll be able to take me. And I'm going to make sure that you are more than ready to before I even think about pushing inside you."

"Oh…" She gasps in surprise.

"You asked to see my heaven, *piscín.*" I gruff as I wrap my arms around her, lift her to my chest, and help wrap her legs around my waist. Carrying her toward my bedroom, I roughly claw my fingertips down her spine. A sweet whimper of pained arousal blows over her lips as her back arches away from my firm touch. The curve causes her bare pussy to grind against the tip of my cock, and I whisper, "But you're going to fucking burn for me first."

Reaching my room, our lips don't part as I climb onto the bed and tenderly press her against the black duvet beneath us. I lightly pin her hands above her head as my lips trail down her neck. Without pausing, I run the tip of my tongue along her collarbone before grazing over it with my teeth, enjoying the change in her whimpers to both the pleasure and the light pain.

As I pepper kisses over her chest, I swirl my tongue around her nipple, mimicking the teasing motion with my fingers on the other. A breathy mewl passes over her sweet lips as I suck her into my mouth and roll her bud between my teeth. I soothe the tender bite with my tongue and release her from my mouth, growling, "I fucking love how responsive you are to my touch. "

My lips and tongue trail between her cleavage and down to her stomach as I continue to palm both her heaving tits. "Your sounds… The feel of your heart thumping against my hands...," I kiss the words along her bikini line. "And the sweet fucking scent of your arousal as I make my way between your thighs."

I trace over her hip bone with my tongue and draw in a deep breath, filling my lungs with her essence. "You're dripping for me," I inform her when I take in the view of her glistening cunt. Teasing us both, I leave a trail of wet kisses over her lightly hair-covered mound. "I need to taste you, *piscín*," I plead, staring over her smooth stomach as my lips run along the crease of her upper thigh.

A feral groan rattles from my lungs as I drag the flat of my tongue from her entrance to her clit. "You taste like fucking heaven," I moan into her pussy as I lap at her, and she spasms beneath me. "Do I need to stop?" I ask, lifting my head.

"No," she breathlessly huffs. When she tries to sit up from the duvet, I'm met with what can only be described as an are-you-fucking-kidding-me face that causes me to chuckle slightly..

I immediately press my face back between her thighs to lick and suck at her, giving her exactly what she wants.. I tease around her clit until she's writhing beneath me. Grabbing her hand from its clutch on the blankets beneath her, I slide her fingers into my hair. "Put me where you want me. Force me to make you come all over my face."

Her hand rests on my head, her fingers laced in my hair as I continue to keep her moments from the brink. She tightens her grip and holds me in place, grinding her hips against my face. Breathy moans blow over her lips as her hard little clit drags along my tongue. My cock aches with need, dampening my boxer briefs with precum from listening to her so close to the edge.

"Let me help you." My muffled words vibrate on her pussy as I rub a finger around her dripping entrance. She's so wet and ready that it slips inside with ease. Pulling back, I add another as her hips buck against my face. *She's so fucking close.* I thrust my fingers slowly, more focused on stretching her than making her come because as much as I want to slam into her, I don't want to hurt her.

Sucking her clit into my mouth, I gingerly work in a third finger, and it's her undoing. Clenched around my digits and writhing against my face, Catlin spasms beneath me as her orgasm fires through her. After I pull my fingers from her, I continue to place wet kisses against her pussy as she rides her high.

Slipping from the bed, I shed my shorts and grab a condom from the bedside table. Her eyes are wide as she watches me roll it over my length. I don't want to keep her waiting, so I climb back onto the bed and settle between her thighs, my throbbing cock resting against the wet warmth of her cunt. Staring down at her gorgeous hazel eyes, I brush her hair from her face and ask, "Are you sure?"

CHAPTER TWENTY-FIVE
CATLIN

"Yes," I whisper. I've never been more sure of anything. Never in my life would I have imagined that the heavily tattooed, intimating man I met a few weeks ago could also be this sweet, gentle, and concerned with my comfort. He isn't what I imagined as a partner, but he's the man that I've been waiting my whole life for. The man worthy of sharing this sacred moment with. "Very."

"I'll be gentle," he promises with his soft blue eyes reassuring me. Reaching between us, Finn aligns himself with me and stills. "Relax, *piscín.* You can take me," he comforts, pressing against me.

Gripping his broad shoulders with both hands, I close my eyes and take a deep breath to relax. A sputtered moan breaks my soft exhale as Finn enters me. I suddenly feel so full, like he barely fits. There's an awkward discomfort of him filling me, but—like he promised—he doesn't hurt me.

"You're doing so good letting me in," Finn croons, continuing to inch his never-ending length into me. Fully seated inside me, he stills his hips and kisses me. He slips his tongue between my lips, which has a foreign slight tang as it teases against mine. I take a minute to realize that I'm tasting the remnants of myself on him—the taste he couldn't get enough of—and I like it. Our tender kiss grows needy, both of us yearning for more. Pulling back, Finn's eyes are filled with need. He flexes his hips, moving inside my channel, and I gasp at the sensation.

"I'll go slowly," Finn promises. Holding my hips to still me, he kisses my neck as he slowly undulates his hips. This feels so different from his fingers, but the fullness of him sliding into me is indescribably good. Finn licks up the length of my neck and over my chin, as he plunges his tongue back into my mouth. He slowly drags his hard length over a spot that causes my back to arch as I moan into his mouth.

"You're so tight, and fuck, do you ever feel good wrapped around me," Finn groans. He bites his lower lip and fists the sheets beside my head. "It's taking everything I have to hold back."

"Don't," I beg, wanting more. *Needing more.* "Show me your heaven."

"Cat," he exhales, dragging my arms over my head. He crosses my wrists and lightly pins them to the mattress. "*You* are my heaven."

Running his free hand over my skin, he drags it along my side and up my thigh. He pulls my leg over his hip, and I let out a breathy grunt as he suddenly sinks even deeper into me. Pinned beneath him with his firm grip holding my leg, he slowly increases the depth and speed of his thrusts. My hips rock to meet his long strokes, and I fist at the sheets beneath my hands as he works me back to that incredible edge. I pant his name, "Finn..."

"That's it," he praises. "Be my good girl and let go. Show me just how much you love the feel of my cock inside you." His teeth graze my breast, and his finger-tips dig into the flesh of my thigh as he pulls me higher. He slides fully into me, and my back arches from the bed as I explode beneath him. The pleasure between my legs shoots through every nerve in my body as my breathy screams fill the room.

"Fuck, *piscín,*" Finn groans as his lips crash against mine. He swallows my cries as I continue to unfurl beneath him. "You look like a fucking angel when you come," he gravelly whispers, pulling back from our kiss.

Finn worships every inch of my body with his lips and hands as he continues to slide his length in and out of me, every touch bringing me a different wave of pleasure. Hovering at the edge of another orgasm, Finn tenderly demands, "Come for me. Squeeze that perfect pussy of yours around my cock as you make me come."

He changes the angle of his hips, and I can't deny his request even if I wanted to. My nails dig into his shoulders as I come harder than I have all night. Driving deep with a roar, Finn's face scrunches with pained relief as his hips sputter against me. His forehead pressed to mine, his warm breath blows over my face as we both struggle to catch our breath.

Finn reaches between us before gently pulling himself from me. He places a soft kiss against my lips and breathlessly whispers, "I'll be right back." Before I can respond, he slips from the bed and retreats to the adjoining bathroom. The water runs briefly, and I glance up to find him in the doorway using a washcloth to clean himself. He tosses it to the floor and grabs another, bringing it with him as he returns to the bed.

"Let me clean you up," he requests, tenderly wiping the cloth along my legs. "You bled a little."

Glancing down, a bit of smeared blood stains my upper thighs and has stained the sheets beneath me. Embarrassed, I mutter, "I'm sorry."

"Absolutely nothing to be sorry or embarrassed about," Finn reassures as he slides back into the bed with me. Pulling me into him, he whispers against my lips, "I love you, *piscín*."

"I love you," I return his whisper as he holds me even tighter into him.

With my head resting on his chest, he places soft kisses against my forehead and strokes my hair. "Are you okay?"

"Very," I lightly chuckle, still high on bliss.

Finn pulls the blanket over us, and we nuzzle beneath it. We lay in near silence, simply enjoying the feel of being pressed to one another with our limbs intertwined.

Rolling into him and resting my chin on his chest, I break the silence. "Can I ask you something?"

"Cat, baby, you can ask me anything."

CHAPTER TWENTY-SIX
CATLIN

"The club?" My voice is soft as I muster through my question. "Is that the kind of things you like?"

Delicately pushing me from his chest, Finn rolls onto his side until we are facing each other. With my hands on his chest and his resting on my hip, his answer is honest. "That depends on what you saw."

"I saw *a lot*."

"One at a time then." He gives a gentle nod for me to ask away.

"Watching? Or being the one they're watching?"

"Yes," he answers quickly, with no need to think about it.

"Oh..." I let out a little gasp, quickly gathering my thoughts. While walking that hallway felt dirty and wrong, there was something arousing and exciting about it as well.

"It's not something you need to do tomorrow." He rubs his thumb over my hip bone. "Or ever, if you aren't comfortable. Both watching or being watched."

"I kind of enjoyed watching. It was… Just, it was a lot."

There's a glimmer in his eyes, and his voice is laced with a tinge of excitement. "What else did you see?"

Thinking back on the acts I briefly saw, I recount the man with the same paddle Sister Francine had at boarding school—and how it only took one strike to never want to upset her again. "The paddles?"

"*Piscín*, I would never want to hurt that gorgeous ass of yours." His hand slides over my hip, and he firmly cups the cheek of my butt. "That's definitely Liam's thing," he shares, and I can feel my brows scrunch in confusion.

Liam seems so sweet.

"There was a woman tied to some sort of bench." I recall the woman completely helpless as a man had his way with her so roughly that tears painted her cheeks.

"Never," he reassures me, as though he knew exactly what window I was referring to.

"I don't get off on impact play—the paddles—or the

idea of having you tied up. I have different needs," he informs me. "More primitive. Primal."

I stare back at him, not sure what to ask but wanting to know more.

"Teeth. Digging my fingers into your flesh. Nails." He cocks a brow and looks at his shoulder, drawing attention to the deep scratches from my nails. "How you nearly drew blood when you clawed at my skin as you came."

I run my fingers over the tender marks I didn't know I had inflicted on him.

"I don't want you bound in submission. I want you to fight, make me chase you down, and overpower you as I take what I want. Taking you the way we both secretly know you want me to."

I swallow hard. "Like after the club in the park?"

Finn answers with a needy growl, "Exactly like the fucking park."

"You liked chasing me?"

"In that moment, no," he answers. "I was worried about losing you, what you'd seen, and how hurt you were. But yes, in different circumstances, I would've happily ripped off your panties and fucked you raw in the grass."

A flush creeps over my cheeks as I remember being forcefully pinned beneath him, my heart racing with fear and adrenaline. In that moment, I hated him, but there was something else about it. *Something I liked.* Even now, I can't deny the effect that thinking of him hunting me down has on me.

"Conor?"

"Gross. I'm definitely not into the idea of fucking Conor in the grass." Finn feigns absolute disgust. "Or even remotely at all."

"No." I laugh, lightly slapping his chest. "I saw Conor."

"Not into that either," he quips. "Watching my brothers is... just... weird."

"He was with a woman and another man. She was... With both of them... At the same time," I struggle through describing what was happening between them.

"I have done that before," he answers honestly.

"Oh." The disparaged word falls from my mouth, knowing with certainty that is something I could never give him.

"That was with women who didn't matter to me," he clarifies. "I would *never* share you. I'm going to make sure the whole fucking world knows that I am the only man who will *ever* have the pleasure of the salvation found in the heaven nestled between your thighs."

Did he just say what I think he did?

"Ever?"

Tucking a tendril of hair behind my ear, he imparts, "An eternity in heaven wouldn't be long enough."

"I lo—" My words are silenced as he abruptly rolls on top of me and crashes his lips into mine. He claims my mouth with renewed virility, taking my breath away as I feel him growing hard against me.

"I need more of you," Finn groans, his words vibrating against my lips when he breaks our kiss. Shifting his weight and reaching between us, Finn rubs his hand up my inner thigh. "Are you sore? Or can I worship you again?"

I slide my hands along the muscles of his back as he rubs teasing circles around my entrance as I stare up at him. "Only if you show me—"

Finn plunges two fingers into me, and a grunt erupts from me. "Show you what, *piscín*?"

His fingers thrust and curl inside of me, quickly leaving me breathless. "How you really like it."

"Don't make a sound as you come all over my hand and I'll show you everything." His gruff promise confuses me, but I nod as he continues to work his fingers into me. He's firm and aggressively demanding my orgasm. I bury my face in my chest, hoping to muffle my whimpers and moans as he diligently works me to the edge. He grinds his palm over my clit, but I can't hold back. Needing to scream, I sink my teeth into the flesh of his pec to silence my screams, and an animalistic growl rattles beneath my lips.

"Good fucking girl," he gravelly whispers as he rolls from me and rubs his arousal-coated fingers over the deep red marks I left within the ink on his chest. He quickly rolls on a condom and sinks into me, burying himself deep. He fills me with long, deep strokes. "Show me what a good fucking girl you are as I make you come again."

CHAPTER TWENTY-SEVEN
FINNIGAN

With both of us exhausted from our lack of sleep—and wanting to keep her to myself—I tried relentlessly to convince Catlin to stay in bed with me this morning. While I nearly swayed her, she was adamant about getting back to help set up for the baptism this morning.

"He's going to be wandering the grounds any minute now, and he can't see me like this." Catlin quickly climbs from the car without waiting for me to get to her door. "I'll call you when we're done."

We're going to need to talk about that.

She looks fucking adorable, racing up the steps. She swims in my T-shirt and is clutching the waistband of my grossly too-large sweatpants to keep them from falling from her petite frame.

Reaching over the car console, I grab the bag containing her wet clothes and sneakers before climbing from the Bronco. I take my time walking up the steps and let myself into the church. Walking toward the altar, I offer my genuflection when I reach the front pew. I place the bag of her clothes on the well-worn wood and sit beside it as I wait for her.

When she enters from the hallway near the altar, Catlin's eyes go wide upon seeing me sitting in the pew. Scuffling toward me, she exclaims, "What are you doing here?"

"Isn't this where I return your panties." I smirk, tapping the bag beside me. "Also, you fo—"

"Catlin?" Father O'Flaherty's voice calls from where she entered from. "Did I hear you come in?"

"You can't be here." She fists the front of my shirt, and I let her drag me from the pew. His footsteps grow louder, and she pulls me into the confessional and quickly shuts the door before Father O'Flaherty spots us together. She whisper-shouts, "You could've returned my panties later."

"I could have." I shrug. "But I also didn't get to kiss you goodbye."

"We're going to get caught"— she abruptly pauses when Father O'Flaherty's footsteps cause the floor just beyond the confessional door to creak—"because you didn't get to kiss me."

"I'm willing to risk far more than getting caught for you, *piscín*." A slightly annoyed look of defeat washes over her face. Closing what little distance there is between us in this tight space, I run my fingers down the buttons of her short-sleeved cardigan and dip them into the waistband of her navy dress skirt. "You clean up nice, and you look almost as beautiful as you did splayed across my bed this morning."

"Fine. Kiss me goodbye." A smirk pulls at her lips, but her eyes give her away.

Dropping the bag of wet clothes into the corner, I cup her face. I lean close enough to feel her breath flutter over my lips before stopping. Without breaking our gaze, I take my time kneeling on the familiar worn green velvet of the prayer bench.

"You said you were going to kiss me!" Catlin quietly exclaims as I inch her tight navy skirt up her toned thighs.

"I did." With the skirt over her hips and bunched around her waist, I hook my fingers under her panties and drag them down her legs. "I just didn't say where."

"Finn," she exhales my name, pulling back from me until she's resting against the ledge behind her. I grab her left leg and lift it over my shoulder to spread her wider for me. Bending her knee, she digs her heel into my back, pulling me into her as she lightly protests, "This is a house of worship."

"And I'm on my knees, *piscín*." I kiss along the thigh draped over my shoulder, and her breath hitches when I reach the tender spot of her upper thigh. "Eager and ready to pray for my spot in heaven."

Gripping her ass, I run the tip of my tongue through her sweet pussy. She lets out a string of breathy grunts when I repeatedly flick over her clit. Lacing her fingers into my hair, she pulls me into her and grinds herself against my mouth. My cock throbs as my sweet, innocent girl sinfully rides my tongue and beautiful whimpers fill the confines of our confessional.

Fuck...

Reaching up, I cup her breast and squeeze the tight nipple pressing against her cardigan. I swirl my tongue around her clit, and a loud moan slips over her lips. "You need to be quiet, *piscín*," I remind her, pulling back.

Her hand slides from my hair, and she grips the prayer ledge as I continue to worship at her altar. Arousal drips down my chin as I continue to feast on her, keeping her on the edge because I can't get enough of her taste on my tongue. The foot pressing against my back flexes, and her thighs begin to tremble as she teeters on the verge of her release.

Squeezing the ledge in her hands so hard it must hurt, her head falls back, and a breathy scream blows over her lips as her hips buck against my face. She comes hard and long; the release continuing to spasm through her as I relentlessly suck and lick at her sensitive clit.

After she's come down, I slip her leg from my shoulder; her legs are unsteady as I pull her dress back over her hips and down her thighs. Rising before her, I use her panties to clean her arousal from my face as she struggles to catch her breath.

"I would give these back"—I dangle the panties in my hand before her as I grab her hand and pull it to my throbbing cock—"But I'm going to need them when I get home." An adorable embarrassment creeps over her already-flushed cheeks as I tuck them into my pocket.

Placing a chaste kiss against her lips, I turn the knob and crack the door to ensure the coast is clear before stepping out of the tiny wooden closet. "You'll have to let me know later if that earned me a spot in heaven," I whisper before closing the door.

CHAPTER TWENTY-EIGHT
CATLIN

ONE WEEK LATER

Even in my dreams, I can't get enough of Finn's face between my thighs. I can still feel him licking me when the orgasm wakes me.

Lucky for me, I think he enjoys it even more than I do.

A sharp nip at my inner thigh abruptly pulls me from my groggy state, and I throw back the covers to find Finn staring back at me wearing a devilish grin. Arching a brow, he chirps, "Good morning."

"Finn!"

"Yes, that *is* what you were screaming as you came."

Playfully slapping at him, I huff. "You can't sneak in here and wake me up like... *that!*"

"I can." He smirks. "And I did. And you came so fucking hard that you soaked your sheets, *piscín*."

Laying in a damp puddle of my arousal, I can't even argue with him as he kisses up my body. Finn grabs a condom from the bedside table and tears it open with his teeth as I fret, "If Uncle Sean catches you here..."

"Then we better hurry." Finn tears his T-shirt from my body and rolls me until I'm face-down beneath him. Grabbing my hips, he lifts them from the mattress as he slides into me. His first few strokes are slow and deep, giving me a chance to adjust to him inside me. As though he knows when I'm ready, he picks up his pace until his hips are relentlessly slamming against me. "Fuck, I love watching that ass of yours jiggle as I fuck you from behind."

Sex with Finn—*of which there's been a lot of this past week*—is always a surprise. He can be so gentle and tender, worshipping me until we're both beyond exhaustion. Other times, he's absolutely feral in the way he takes me.

Like him, I can't get enough of either...

"Finn," I groan as he has me dangling at the edge of my release so quickly. The headboard bangs against the wall from his vigorous thrusts as I claw at the sheets beneath me. His fingertips dig into my hips as he tries to take me faster, so hard that his short nails dimple my flesh. Needing desperately to come, I arch my back and push into him. "Please…"

"So fucking needy," he teases, reaching over me to take my hand. He drags it beneath us and presses both our hands between my thighs. Slamming into me from behind, he rubs my fingers over my clit, quickly pulling my orgasm from me. "That's it," he encourages. "Come all over my cock."

He firmly fists my butt cheek, and I wince in pain, exploding when he slams into me again. My hips spasm, and it's all I can do to bite the pillow to silence my screams as my thighs tremble so hard that I collapse against the mattress. Grabbing my hands, he presses them to the rocking headboard as he continues to drive into me without abandon.

"You're mine, *piscín*," Finn growls as he bites at the back of my shoulder. His teeth sink deep into my flesh, and it hurts so good that I nearly come again. He sucks at the tender skin, and I moan with pleasure as he leaves his bruising mark. Sloppily kissing over the mark to soothe it, he grunts through his thrusts, "Mine. All. Of. You. Is. Mine."

"Yours," I pant as he roughly bites my other shoulder.

His hips sputter against me, and he thrusts the entirety of himself into me to bury himself to the hilt. Nipping at his newest mark, he fills the condom with a guttural groan. Spent and buried inside my pussy, he tenderly kisses my tender flesh up my neck. His lips dust along my ear, and he purrs, "I'm going to mark every fucking inch of you, so everyone knows that you're mine."

"You could just tattoo your name over that handprint I'm pretty sure you left on my butt," I brat.

"*Piscín,* nothing would make me happier than permanently marking you as mine." Shocked, I roll onto my back as he pulls from me, I stare at his chest. The silhouette of a black cat runs the length of his sternum—over his heart—marking him as mine.

"Returning the favor only seems fair." I smirk, running my fingers over his newest tattoo and watching his eyes light up. Shaking my head, I clarify, "but not on my butt."

Marking my body isn't the only thing I want to reciprocate.

Tossing the condom in the trash, Finn pulls on his boxer briefs and pants before climbing back into the bed with me. Tenderly, he hovers over me, kissing along my collarbone and up my neck before claiming my mouth once more. His lips linger against mine as I whisper, "You should go. Before we get caught."

"We're going to have to break the news to him, eventually." Finn begrudgingly climbs from the bed and picks his shirt off the floor.

"Yes," I agree. "But eventually isn't going to be with me naked and you half-dressed in the convent."

After pulling my sheets from the bed and shoving them into the washing machine, I take a quick shower. I dry myself off and grab my phone while still wrapped in my towel, reaching out for some help with an issue that has been plaguing me for a few days.

> Do you have a few minutes to talk?

I put on a cute floral sundress—and then a thin cardigan to cover the bites and hickeys across my shoulders—giving some time for the recipient to reply.

> LAYLA
> Of course!

I type and delete my response several times before pressing the button to call her instead.

"You've been typing for five minutes." Layla chuckles when she answers the phone. "What's up?"

"This is so embarrassing," I admit. "I want to... with my mouth, but I don't know how."

"I don't know if I should be honored or offended that I'm your first call for advice on sucking cock," Layla quips. "But you've come to the right place." She gives me a short list of what to do and what not to do, before going into explicit details of technique.

"So help me if that's one of my brothers, *mo cuishle.*" Tristan's deep voice billows through the speakerphone.

"All of them, actually," she brats. "We're planning a gangbang for my birthday."

I don't know if I want to know what that is...

CHAPTER TWENTY-NINE
FINNIGAN

While I sit in the club's lounge with Conor and Declan, we go over the prior month's financials as we wait for Tristan and Liam to arrive.

"What have you done to that sweet, innocent girl of yours?" Tristan jests, slapping my back, when he joins us.

Caught off-guard by his question, I retort, "I'm going to need you to be a tad more specific."

"She was on the phone with Layla when I left," Tristan shares.

"And?" I snark, knowing that the two of them talk all the time.

"Three things… First, I learned way more than I needed to know about how much pussy you eat. But it tracks with how much you run your mouth. Second,

I'm looking into Panty Sniffer Anonymous options for you," he jests.

Jesus Christ, these girls talk about absolutely everything with one another.

"That's rich, coming from the panty stealer," I quip, recalling him removing all of Layla's from her apartment to ensure she was always panty-free. "Also, it definitely doesn't need to be anonymous. I fucking love the scent of her. I'd happily carry her little cotton panties in my pocket."

"I swear I learn shit about you every fucking day that I didn't want to." Declan gruffs.

"I'm sorry," Conor chimes, ticking up his hand to draw my attention. "Did you say little cotton panties? Because fuck, that's hot."

"Nuh-uh." I shake my head at him, severely disapproving of what I imagine him doing with that information. "You can keep Catlin and her panties out of your thoughts."

"Too late." He sighs. "Are we talking about plain white ones? Or maybe those cute little flowery ones?"

Fighting the urge to beat the piss out of him, I snarl, "I swear to fucking God—"

"Don't stop," Declan goads him with a wicked smirk. "I'm really fucking enjoying watching him on the receiving end for a change."

"Fuck the lot of you." I sneer at both of them before turning my attention to Tristan. "And the third thing?"

"Let's just say Layla was giving her a *very* detailed lesson on the many things Catlin can use her mouth for."

Such a naughty little girl she is.

My cock twitches at the thought of her wrapping her lips around it.

"I got stuck in traffic," Liam announces as he walks into the club. "What'd I miss?"

Standing from his seat and walking behind me, Declan condescendingly pats me on the head. "Our baby brother is finally going to get his cock sucked."

Over-exaggerating an adjustment of his cock, Conor shares, "And I bet Catlin will look fucking incredible on her knees in nothing more than her little white cotton briefs."

"That's fucking it," I roar, rising from my seat so abruptly that it scoots across the floor. I lunge at Conor, toppling his chair and taking us both to the ground with a hefty thud before landing a punch onto his jaw.

Ignoring the two of us wrestling across the floor, Tristan says, "When you two fucks are done, we need to talk about the Pakhan."

The Pakhan?

The word draws my and Conor's attention, ceasing our scuffle. We haven't seen or heard from him or the Bratva in months. Not since the night I shot him when we forced our way into the apartment in Brighton Beach to get Quinn back. Shoving away from one another, Conor and I both climb from the floor and retake our seats around the table.

"Rory called me on my way over and informed me that one of the guys under him saw the Pakhan at a bar uptown last night."

"How sure are we?" Declan asks, his tone pained with worry. The Bratva have already tried to take Quinn from him twice. He'd burn the city to the ground before letting any of them ever lay a hand on her again.

"Sure enough," Tristan answers. "Until we know otherwise, it's not worth the risk to assume it wasn't him."

A sense of dread washes over me, suddenly realizing how lax I've been—*we've all been*—the past couple of months. We've stopped traveling in groups, leaving all of us at risk. Tris only has two men on his building and chauffeuring Layla around the city now. Even the army surrounding Declan's house has dwindled back down to a normal security team, with Rory leading the crew.

Fucking foolish idiots, the lot of us.

Especially me. I've made zero arrangements for Catlin's safety. If the two of us can leap over the meager wall separating her home from the city night after night without being detected, the Bratva—*or any enemy*—would be able to get to her with ease. Thoughts of the night they came for Quinn at the bar and anything like that ever happening to Catlin has my stomach churning.

I don't realize that worry is painted across my face, but my brothers all clearly see it. "She'll be fine," Liam assures me, tapping my knee to garner my attention as he pulls his phone from his pocket. "I'm already getting a couple of guys over to the church."

"I don't wa—"

"I'll make sure they're discreet. Neither Catlin nor Father O'Flaherty will have any idea they are there."

"Thank you." I appreciatively tap his arm. "I want to be the one to let her know what kind of danger I've inadvertently put her in."

Danger I hadn't yet realized I'd be putting her in for the rest of her life.

CHAPTER THIRTY

FINNIGAN

Fueled by an unfamiliar nervousness, I head to the church to pick up Catlin much earlier than we had agreed upon. Parking my bike next to our little slab of concrete, I'm pleased to spot two of our guys lingering around the perimeter of the church grounds. While they immediately stand out to me, I highly doubt that they would get a second glance from either Catlin or Father O'Flaherty.

After removing my helmet and climbing from the bike, I pull my phone from my jeans to text Cat.

I'm in our spot, piscín

CATLIN

You're early

I missed you

While it's not a lie—*I miss the fuck out of her when we're apart*—I omit the full truth of being concerned for her safety.

Uncle Sean was actually just leaving.

Subtly, I look up from my phone to see the church van driving toward me with Father O'Flaherty behind the wheel. I attempt to avert my face, hoping he doesn't notice me loitering.

I have to finish up this announcement and lock up

Meet me in the convent in about ten minutes

Realizing she's all alone in that big, empty church, I quickly decide against waiting. *This will be much more fun.* With a smile tugging at my lips, I briskly walk around the block, shooting her a quick response.

See you soon.

Silently taking the church steps two at a time, I quickly reach the landing and crack the main door of the church to ensure she's not in sight. When I find the coast clear, I slip inside, flip off the lights, and slam the door. Papers flutter from the table in the center of the vestibule, and the sound boom echoes down the nave.

"Hello?" Cat calls down the stairs. "Uncle Sean?"

I slink into the narthex and reach the light switches for the main level. Flipping them all, the only remaining light is filtered through the stained-glass windows, leaving shadows cascading down the center of the church to the altar.

Fucking perfect.

The old stairs creak beneath Cat's heels as she takes her time coming downstairs. Her shoes click on the tiled floor in the vestibule, and she timidly calls, "Uncle Sean? Is that you?"

Walking past a table, I push over a candelabra, causing it to clatter to the tiles beneath it. The clang reverberates around the narthex as the candles roll across the floor, and I slip into the shadows in the nave.

"Hello?" Her breathy voice cracks. Her pace slows as she hesitantly makes her way toward me. "Is someone there?"

Grabbing a Bible from the back of a pew, I carry it a few steps before letting it fall to the tile floor with a hearty thud. Catlin's heels scratch across the floor as she spins around with a fear-filled squeak flying from her lungs.

"Uncle Sean?" she tentatively calls in the darkness. "Finn?"

The church is near silent. The only sounds filling the vast space are her increasingly heavy breaths and her hesitant steps as she continues to creep closer to me unknowingly. She stands only feet from where I'm cloaked in the darkness, and for a second, I swear I can hear her heart thumping.

Adrenaline is coursing through her, and the scent of her fear is fucking intoxicating. Taking a silent breath as she passes, I inhale the intoxicating scent. But it isn't all fear I smell. The unmistakable aroma of her arousal that I've been drunk on for weeks is so strong that her panties must be absolutely soaked.

My sweet girl—ever full of surprises—likes this.

Standing in the aisle between the pews, she slowly spins in a circle, trying to find the source of her unease. "Finn..." Her voice is laced with fear when she shouts, "This isn't funny!"

I deepen my voice and gravelly whisper from the darkness, "It isn't supposed to be." Her entire body grows rigid; a devilish chuckle rattles from my lungs and echoes throughout the nave.

Her feet are rooted in place, but she's desperate to run. Catlin swallows hard, the gulp in her throat audible in the distance between us. She takes a step back toward the narthex before abruptly turning and running toward the altar. To the courtyard—where she thinks I'm waiting—in the convent.

Running along the wall of the church, my boots stomp against the tiles with every long stride. I close the distance between us quickly, catching her as she runs past the altar. A terrified scream billows from her when I grab her from behind. Lifting her from the ground, her feet kick against my shins, and she claws at my arms wrapped around her, screaming at me to release her. Her heels fall from her feet, clattering against the tiles as she continues to fight me.

I'm so fucking hard I might burst.

Roughly bending her over the altar, I press my hand to her back and pin her to it. Writhing against my firm hold and playing along, she cries, "What do you want?"

Her heart pounds so hard that it reverberates against my hand pressed to her back as I lightly kick her feet apart. I grab the flowing skirt of her floral dress and toss it over her back, growling at the sight of her new lacy panties. Firmly gripping them, I press my fingers through the fabric and tear them from her.

Dropping to my knees and pressing my face into her from behind, I growl, "To earn my spot in heaven."

CHAPTER THIRTY-ONE

CATLIN

Bending me over the most sacred place in the church, Finn roughly palms my butt as he licks and sucks at my pussy like a starving man. His magical tongue quickly and expertly brings me to the brink. I claw at the cold marble, my cries of pleasure filling the church as he feasts on me. My thighs tremble, and I cling to the altar to stay on my toes as I ride Finn's tongue. "Finnnnn..." My release pulls the words out as a breathless scream.

"Are you praying, *piscín*?" he taunts, licking my arousal from my thighs as he pulls his face from between them. He kisses up the back of my still trembling leg as he stands before lowering my dress. Finn helps me to my unsteady feet as he pulls me into his arms. Crashing his lips into mine, he claims my mouth. Every swipe of his tongue coats it with the taste of my arousal until I'm the only thing I can taste.

"Kneel at my altar." His soft words vibrate against my lips as he breaks our kiss. Staring down at me, he rubs his thumb along my lower lip. "You can worship me with these pouty lips. Or is God the only man you kneel for?"

Holding his gaze, I dart my tongue from between my lips and lick along the tip of his thumb. He presses it into my mouth and he rubs it over my tongue as I close my lips around it. Dragging it from my mouth, he slides the saliva-coated digit over my lips as I kneel before him.

My fingers tremble—showing my nerves—as I work to undo his belt. Finally freeing it, I drop it against him as I undo the button and the zipper of his jeans. He pushes at the top of them, helping me to lower them to his thighs and letting his hard length spring free. I swallow hard as it bobs in front of my face, wondering how I'm actually going to fit all of him into my mouth. "Take what you can," Finn directs, fisting the base of his shaft. A moment later, he rubs the soft skin of his tip along my lips.

Remembering Layla's words from our conversation this morning—"a *good hand job involves your mouth, and a good blow job involves your hands*"—I replace Finn's hand with my own. Holding him gently in my fist, I slide my hand along his length and place wet kisses against the soft skin resting on my lips.

"Your lips feel so good against my cock," Finn groans as he wraps his hand over mine to tighten my grip.

I can do this.

Opening my mouth, I take him past my lips and onto my tongue as I circle my lips around this girthy shaft. Carefully sliding my hand along him, I work the first few inches of him into my mouth.

Breathy grunts rattle from him as I rub my tongue along the underside of his shaft. Running his fingers through my hair, he dusts them down the side of my face and croons, "I wish you could see how fucking beautiful you are on your knees with my cock in your mouth."

He reaches between us and palms my breast as I continue to slide him in and out of my mouth. He rolls my nipple between his fingers, and I groan around my mouthful of him, causing a feral sound to fall from his lips.

Encouraged by the sounds he makes, letting me know how much I'm pleasing him, I bob my head a little faster and take a bit more of him into my already full mouth. When I accidentally take too much, he presses over the back of my tongue, and I gag when he hits my throat.

"Easy, *piscín*," he urges, wiping the spittle from my chin. "As much as I want to slide every inch of me down your tight throat, we have a lifetime for you to learn how to."

Panting and lacing his fingers into my hair, Finn's breathy growls echo around the church as I please him. Even though I'm kneeling before him, as he towers over me, I'm in complete control of him and his pleasure.

"You're doing so fucking good," Finn pants between heavy breaths.

Hollowing my cheeks and sucking as I slide over him, his shaft grows more rigid in my hand and mouth. "Oh. Fuck. *Piscín*. You're going to make me fucking come. Are you going to take my offering in your mouth?" he grits through his teeth.

Looking up at him through my lashes, I nod as I continue to slide him over my tongue. "Fuck," he roars, as his fingers fist my locks. His rigid shaft twitches, abruptly filling my mouth with his viscous, salty release. Not quite prepared from Layla's description earlier, some of his cum trickles over my lips and down my chin as I try to swallow what he's spilling into my mouth. Finn takes my hands and beams down at me with pride as I let him slide from between my lips. "You did so fucking good for me."

Helping me to my feet before he tucks my hands behind my back, stopping me from cleaning my face, and pulls me into him. He drags his tongue along my neck and over my chin—collecting my spittle and his cum—as he makes his way to my lips. Pressing his tongue between them, he smears his taste into my mouth as he kisses me until I'm breathless.

Finn tucks his softening length into his pants as I fix my dress and grab my discarded heels. As he raises his zipper, he smirks. "I'll be sure to tell your teacher you deserve an A plus."

CHAPTER THIRTY-TWO

CATLIN

Finn slips his belt back into the loops on his pants and playfully pulls me into him. I wrap my arms around his waist, and his beautiful blue eyes bore into mine as he smooths my slightly disheveled hair, tucking a lock behind my ear.

"Catlin, what is going on in he—" Uncle Sean's words are cut short as the lights flick on in the nave. Abruptly turning to his voice, I find him standing on the narthex's threshold with Finn's spilled candelabra in his hand.

Oh, crap...

It falls from his grip, and the thud of it hitting the floor echoes around the church as he races down the center aisle. His face reddens, and his eyes become more rage-filled with every step he takes toward us.

Slipping from Finn's embrace, I try to calm him. "Uncle Sea—"

"Catlin, go!" he demands—misinterpreting Finn's hands on me—as he takes his final strides in our direction. Pulling the clerical collar from his shirt and tossing it to the ground, he shouts, "Call the police!"

Uncle Sean's slam against Finn's chest, and he shoves him away from me with such force that he falters backward into the altar. With anger I've never seen in him before, he fists the front of Finn's shirt as he regains his balance. "Lord forgive me..." Uncle Sean snarls as he shoves him back into the altar

Finn's jaw clenches so hard it must hurt as his hands ball into fists by his sides. He is struggling to stand down from this altercation. Uncle Sean swings a punch, and Finn allows it to crash against his jaw. I'm rooted to the spot and unable to do anything to stop them but plead, "Don't! Please. Stop!"

Uncle Sean continues to rush toward Finn, who keeps shoving him away. Refusing to raise a hand to him, Finn takes another slug and insists, "I'm not going to fight you, old man."

"Catlin, go!" Uncle Sean instructs again, grabbing a heavy candlestick from the altar to use as a weapon.

"Uncle Sean! Stop!" My usually timid voice booms over their scuffle. "It isn't what you think. I love him!"

Stepping back from Finn, he shakes his head in disbelief. "You don't love him."

"I do." I tentatively make my way to stand between the two of them. Taking my place beside Finn, I slip my hand into his large one and intertwine our fingers. "I love him."

"I told you to stay away from him. And his family." His tone shows his displeasure as he shakes his head.

"They're not bad people, Uncle Sean," I softly inform him as I squeeze Finn's hand. "Finn is an amazingly good guy who occasionally does bad things to protect the people he loves."

"You don't know who they really are," Uncle Sean argues. "The good girl I raised wouldn't be stupid enough to let people deceive her."

"Raised?" I huff. "You didn't raise me. You shipped me halfway around the world and shoved me into a boarding school. I was raised by nuns and *Máthair Dhríonna!*"

"Is that what this is?" he snips. "You have daddy issues because I couldn't raise you after my brother died? So, you open your whorish legs for the first man that pays you the slightest bit of attentio—"

"Don't," Finn warns, stepping chest-to-chest with Uncle Sean. Tears well in my eyes from his hateful words. "I know how you feel about me and my family.

I'll let you speak ill of us to feel better about yourself in your home. But if you so much as think about disrespecting her again, you will be lucky only to find yourself on your ass."

"Finn," I sob, squeezing his hand. He steps back from Uncle Sean and turns to find tears streaming down my face.

"*Piscín*," he whispers, swiping his hand across my cheek to gather my salty droplets. His eyes soften, clearly hating to see me in pain, and he tenderly pulls me against him to comfort me.

"This isn't like you. You're a good girl, Catlin," Uncle Sean insists as he watches the two of us. "You listen and do as you're told."

A lifetime of doing everything that has been asked of me, with one solitary decision made for myself. Following the word of the church to a T, I only learned in the past few weeks that love and acceptance have limitations. *For them.*

It's not what I want. At least not anymore.

"Maybe I'm not your good girl anymore," I snark, noting the smug smile Finn is trying to fight from spreading across his face.

"I won't condone this," Uncle Sean gruffs. Digging in his heels, he threatens, "You aren't welcome in my church if you are going to choose *him* and this life of corruption and sin he is going to bestow upon your soul."

Frozen in place, I stare back at Uncle Sean in disbelief as I try to determine whether his words are an idle threat or if he'll truly toss away the only family he has over his deep-rooted hatred of the man I am in love with.

As though he can read my thoughts, Finn pulses my hand, reassuring me. "Don't do this to her. Don't make her choose between the two of us."

Unwavering in his stance, Uncle Sean glares at me and Finn as he awaits my decision. A satisfied smile pulls at Uncle Sean's lips as I slip my hand from Finn's and step away from him.

Glancing over my shoulder at Finn, I cross the altar toward my uncle. "I'm sorry." I hold back a sob as I press onto my toes and place a chaste kiss against his cheek.

CHAPTER THIRTY-THREE
FINNIGAN

"I'm sorry." Catlin places a kiss on her uncle's cheek. Lowering from her tiptoes to her heels, she stares at him and lightly cries, "I'm sorry your hatred for him is greater than your love for me."

Crossing the altar, Catlin slips her hand back into mine, and I give it a reassuring squeeze. Tenderly, I slip my finger under her chin, tipping her face toward mine. "Go get your bag and your phone from upstairs, *piscín*. I'll be right behind you."

I had a brief moment of doubt that she would allow him to make this choice for her—*as he has with nearly every decision about her life*—when her dainty hand slid from mine. That crushing fear flittered away the second she glanced over her shoulder at me, her eyes telling me everything I needed to know.

She will choose me.

Always.

My name is tattooed across her heart as deeply as hers is over mine. She could relive this moment in a thousand lifetimes and still choose me. I give her something that he never could… I love her for who she is and provide her with the freedom to grow as she sees fit. She doesn't have to hide her fears and desires from me because I willingly accept them all, shouldering some of the burden I know she feels. I want her to flourish into the gorgeous creature she was meant to be. In choosing us, she's finally choosing *herself.*

And I'm so fucking proud of her.

"I told you not to make her choose." I huff, shaking my head at Father O'Flaherty once Catlin is out of earshot. "Either option was going to break her heart."

Still floored by her decision, he has no retort or snide remark about her. *Or me.* When I walk to the aisle, I pause for a second and turn back to him. "I hope we both see you soon, for Catlin's sake."

By the time I make my way down the long aisle, Catlin is traversing the last of the stairs. She glances toward the doorway leading into the nave when she reaches the bottom step and sniffles as she half-heartedly jokes, "You didn't kill him, did you?"

"No. I very politely let him know he's a fucking idiot." Cupping her face as she reaches me, I place a soft kiss against her lips and whisper, "Let's get you home, *piscín*."

Home.

Our home.

She's quiet as I lead her from the church and around the block to where I parked my bike. "It'll be okay," I promise, pulling the helmet over her head and doing the strap. The big white helmet bobs as she nods, her eyes still pained and teary as I close the visor.

I fucking hate seeing her like this.

I nod at the guys watching the church, silently letting them know they don't need to follow and that I've got Cat. Owen discreetly lifts and lightly shakes his phone, urging me to read the messages incessantly vibrating over the last few minutes. Pulling it from the back pocket of my pants, I quickly key in my code to read his message.

OWEN

The same black SUV has passed the church four times this past hour

Slowing each time at your bike and the entrance

Definitely Bratva behind the wheel

"Is something wrong?" Cat's concerned voice is muffled by her helmet.

"Just letting my brothers know I can't help them tonight." I omit the truth as I send them a message. I'll inform her about the Bratva threats later. She's dealing with enough right now. Adding them to things definitely isn't going to make this any easier.

> Bratva is on to Our Lady of Grace

> I have Cat. Taking her to my place for good.

Swiping back to Owen's message, I send a quick reply before shoving my phone back into my pocket and climbing onto the bike.

> Keep an eye on the church and Father O'Flaherty.

Catlin clings to me tightly as we ride through the city. I wish I'd been in a car so that I could comfort her more than a meager squeeze of her thigh at traffic lights. Reaching the garage to my building, I pull into a spot beside my Bronco and take Cat's hand to help her dismount. Cat fumbles with the strap of her helmet, so I reach under her chin to help. Pulling it from her, I notice that while her eyes are still red, her tears have subsided.

We walk from the garage to my—*our*—apartment with our fingers intertwined. This isn't how I wanted to start this chapter of our lives together, but a selfish part of me is really fucking happy to know that I'm going to have her in my bed each and every night.

Leading her through the apartment, I pull her toward the leather couch and into my lap as I sit. She curls her legs and nestles her face against my chest. Holding her in silence, I stroke her hair and give her a little time to process everything she's feeling. Her fingers dust over my chest, and her voice is soft when she finally speaks. "Finn…"

"Yes, *piscín*?"

"I love you," she whispers. "Your life, it doesn't scare me."

"I love you." Wrapping my arms tighter around her, I kiss her forehead and whisper to myself, "It should."

As I run my fingers along the bare skin of her arm, I glance down and notice the fresh bruises marring her usually perfect porcelain skin. I must've grabbed her harder than I thought at the church. "Did I hurt you?" I ask, lightly rubbing over her tender skin.

CHAPTER THIRTY-FOUR
CATLIN

Finn presses against a freshly forming bruise I didn't realize I had, and his voice is pained. "Did I hurt you?"

For a man who has repeatedly left marks on me with his teeth and mouth—insistently keeping me marked as his—he is grossly concerned with the tiny fingertip imprints forming on my bicep. I lift my head from his chest to find his eyes filled with worry and remorse. Cupping his face, I demand his attention. "I didn't even realize. You didn't hurt me, Finn. I know that you would never hurt me on purpose."

He grips my hips and turns me across his lap so I'm straddling him. His lips are on the little bruises the second he can reach them, tenderly kissing over each mark he left behind.

"If we're going to continue to play like we did today,

you need a safeword," he informs me, his tone immediately becoming very serious.

"A safeword?" I don't understand what he's saying.

"Yes, a safeword," he repeats himself. "A word you wouldn't say while we're playing rough or during sex. It's your way of letting me know that you're not okay. If I hurt you or something makes you feel unsafe, you say it. The moment it passes over your lips, everything is a full stop, and my entire focus is on making sure you don't feel that way any longer."

I nod, acknowledging what he's explaining while simultaneously wondering if he'll ever push me so far that I actually need to use it.

"I can't just say, 'stop?'"

"No." He shakes his head. "Do you know how many times you screamed for me to stop or let you go this afternoon in the church?"

Silently thinking back and recalling him pinning me to the altar, I begin to realize his point. "A lot."

"Had you truly needed me to stop, I wouldn't have known," he admits. "And I would never forgive myself for going too far. That's why you need a word that stands out."

"Okay," I agree. "What kind of word?"

"People use all sorts of things," he shrugs. "Pineapple. Oklahoma. Pickles. Derek Jeter—"

"The baseball player?" I interrupt with a chuckle.

"Yes." His tone softens, and he smiles. "You can choose whatever word you want. It just needs to be something that you'll remember."

Suddenly completely blank on my vocabulary, I stare at him for a minute as I try to think of a word.

"Church."

"Church?" Finn repeats it back to me with an inquisitive brow.

"Yes, church," I insist before explaining, "You said the point of it is to bring me from a not-good place to somewhere I feel safe. Centered. That has always been church for me."

"Then it's perfect," Finn praises, palming my face and pulling me close to press his lips to mine.

His eyes still harbor concern when he pulls back and I ask, "What's wrong?"

"I've never hidden the kind of man I am or the life I lead." He lets out a heavy breath. "But there are details about how it also affects you that we really haven't discussed. Things we need to."

Finn rests his hands on my hips and explains everything that has transpired between the Russian Bratva and his family. The details are so explicit that my heart breaks several times for Quinn and what she has endured to be part of his family.

"Do I need to worry about my safety?" My voice is laced with apprehension and concern.

"Yes," Finn answers honestly. "I shot the head of the Bratva when we went after Quinn. They're fucking cowards, and they'd take you because they can't get to me. But I won't let that happen. Like Layla and Quinn, any time you aren't with me, you'll have guys with you."

"Like Rory?" I clarify, confirming my recent suspicion that he is definitely *more* than a chauffeur.

Finn nods his answer. "You are safe with me, always. I would burn this city to the ground and walk through hell to keep you from harm. And so would my brothers."

After having heard what they went through—and that Conor took a bullet—to bring Quinn home, I don't doubt him. Their family—*my family now*—are so very close and would clearly do anything for one another.

"Sorry, *piscín*," Finn apologizes when his phone rings, and he lifts it from the end table. "I can ignore a text or two, but if they're calling, I have to take this."

He answers the call, roughly grabbing at my hip and pulling me back onto him with his free hand when I attempt to climb from his lap to give him a little privacy.

"Yes, I'm fine. We're fine." He huffs as Declan's muffled voice of annoyance comes through the phone. "If the lot of you had Cat straddling your lap without any panties on, you wouldn't answer the phone either."

"I sure fucking wouldn't." Conor's voice billows through the speaker clear as day. My cheeks instantly flush, leaving me unsure if my embarrassment is from his overt interest or how much Finn shares with them.

"Someone beat the piss out of him for me," Finn barks before hanging up and tossing the phone back onto the table.

"How long have you been thinking about me not having panties on?" I tease.

Gripping both my hips and dragging me up his thighs, Finn confesses, "About the time I realized that sweet, pantyless pussy of yours was vibrating against the leather of my motorcycle seat."

CHAPTER THIRTY-FIVE
FINNIGAN

"Fuck, *piscín*. You look incredible!" I exclaim when Catlin walks into the living room, my eyes hungrily raking over her frame.. Every inch of the body I can't get enough of is showcased in her form-fitted black dress with a plunging—yet somehow modest—neckline. Crossing the room, I pull her into me and kiss along her neck. "So fucking good that I just want to tear that dress from you to find out what you're hiding underneath."

"That's not working again." She places two hands on my chest and shoves me away from her with a smirk. "Last night, you managed to get out of taking me to the club with sex. I haven't been anywhere but this apartment or Quinn's place in a week. I know you're trying to keep me safe, Finn, but I *need* to go somewhere and do something."

"Trust me. If we stay here, we will most definitely be doing something."

Leaning against the kitchen island, Cat's lower lip protrudes in an adorable pout—reminiscent of the one Fiona uses to get her way with Declan—and she pleads, "You promised, Finn."

Fuck... Do they teach them this shit in the womb?

"Give me your shoes." I sigh, extending my hand to take her strappy heels before kneeling at her feet to help her put them on. As I affix the buckle on the second, I run my fingers up the length of her body as I stand. She turns to grab her purse from the counter, and I quickly wrap my arms around her. Her back crashes into my chest with enough force that a small gasp falls from her as I splay my hand across her stomach. Pressing my lips to the shell of her ear, I whisper, "I'll give in and take you to the club, *piscín*. Just know that in return, I'm fucking you when and where I please, with you wearing nothing but these heels later."

Her breath hitches, sputtering as she releases it. My hand slides from her stomach and over her hip. I inhale the sweet, musky scent of her arousal as I kiss her neck. "You like the idea of me taking what's mine, don't you?"

Giving a gentle nod, she whimpers when I nip at the crook of her neck before softly answering, "Yes."

"I can smell you soaking your panties just thinking about it," I gravelly whisper as I inch her dress up her thighs.

"Finn." She grips my hand in protest. "You promised."

"We're going to the club, *piscín*." I continue to work the fabric up her legs. Hooking my fingers under the thin straps of lace covering her, I drag her panties down her legs as I fix her dress into place. "You're just going without panties, so I can spend the night inhaling your essence as it drips down your creamy thighs."

Cat lifts her feet, and I carefully slip the lace from her, ensuring not to tear it. Crumpling them in my palm as I rise to my feet, I feel how soaked they are already. I bring them to my face and breathe in her sweet aroma with a growl before shoving them into my pocket.

My hand rests on Cat's bare thigh during the ride to the club in my Audi. After pulling into the valet, I wave off the attendant when he reaches for her door. Quickly rounding the car, I take her hand and help her from the low seat. She draws the attention of men —*and women*—as we walk inside, her arm tucked into the bend of my elbow. *I* can barely keep my eyes from the stunning, pantyless beauty pressed against me.

She doesn't just fit into my world; she was fucking made for it.

"How does it feel?" I whisper into her ear as we walk into the lounge.

She glances up at me with a tinge of confusion. "How does what feel?"

"Knowing that everyone staring either wants to fuck you or be you," I reply, immediately enjoying the heated blush that rushes over her cheeks. As we pass by a table, a beautiful brunette overtly eyes both me and Catlin, prompting me to add, "Or both."

She squeezes my bicep as we make our way through the crowded room to a table at the back where Tristan, Layla, and Conor are waiting.

"Fucking hell. *Cailín álainn*," Conor exhales, standing as we approach and quickly pulling her in for a hug and a—*too friendly*—kiss on the cheek. "You look fucking incredible."

Growling, I tear her from Conor's hold and stare at him before dragging her onto my lap as I sit. "Get the thought out of your head," I warn Conor and gesture at Tris and Layla, "because *that* isn't happening."

Conor quips, "Cat's on this new journey of making her own decisions. Why don't you let her decide?"

Getting comfortable on my lap, Cat timidly asks, "Decide what?"

My brothers and I stare at her, each of us clearly trying to find the words to answer her question.

"For Christ's sake," Layla blurts when none of us speak. "No need to tiptoe around it. Conor is asking if you'd be open to him sharing you with Finn."

I stare at Layla for a second. I'm about to ask another question and show my ignorance when I remember the night I followed Finn here. Looking through the window to find Conor having a—*very vigorous*—go at a woman as she pleased another man with her mouth.

With my cheeks on fire, I adamantly shake my head. "No. Absolutely not."

"Your loss." Conor shrugs, winking at Layla.

My eyes dart between Conor and Tristan before focusing on Layla, and I gasp. "The three of you?"

"Just once. I was curious," she admits with a shrug before chuckling, "and these guys will literally do anything for their brothers."

"Except me." Finn pulls me tight. "No matter how much they beg, I'd never fucking share you."

Enjoying drinks—*with me occasionally taking tiny sips of Finn's spicy beverage*—the five of us sit in the lounge for a couple of hours. The once-busy room is now only scattered tables of members, with most of the previous occupants having made their way further into the club.

Finn finishes the whiskey in his glass and places it on the table. Dipping his fingers into it, a mischievous grin spreads across his face as he retrieves an ice cube. He holds it between his fingers and wraps his lips around the cube, lightly sucking on it for a few seconds as drips of melting ice trickle down his palm. After pulling it out, he places his frosty lips against the crook of my neck, sending an excited shiver down my spine. His warm breath blows over the icy kiss like fire as he teasingly rubs the cube over my knee.

My heart races as Finn pushes the ice along my inner thigh, leaving a wet trail of goosebumps as he slowly makes his way under the hemline of my dress. Kissing along my neck, he inches the quickly melting cube toward my warm center.

"Not out here," Tristan barks, and I startle, suddenly realizing that we aren't alone as Finn's hand quickly retreats from beneath my dress.

"C'mon, Tris!" Conor playfully whines, only furthering my embarrassment when I notice how fixated he is on me.

"As much as Conor is *clearly* enjoying your show," Tristan continues, "you have to follow the same rules as everyone else, Finn. No play in the lounge."

Dropping the remnants of the cube into the empty whiskey glass in front of us, Finn wipes his damp fingers over the thigh of his pants. Now dry, he slides them along my jaw to draw my attention to him. "Are you ready to play with me, *piscín?*" he whispers with his lips against my ear. I give a trepidatious nod as I stand from his lap, immediately drawing the attention of our table companions.

"Don't do anything I wouldn't." Layla winks as Finn rises and takes my hand. Smiling at her, I shake my head, realizing that I don't think I'd do half the things she has done.

Her comfort with sex still amazes me.

With Finn leading me through the crowded club, we enter the voyeur hall. It is much busier than the night I snuck in here, with people standing shoulder-to-shoulder, watching the couples—*and groups*—at play on the other side of the windows before them.

The first window we pause at has a woman kneeling, her wrists bound to her ankles. She winces as her partner places metal clips between her thighs. Tears trickle down her face as he applies another, and I quickly divert my gaze, unable to watch her in pain.

Squeezing Finn's hand, I nudge him with my shoulder, letting him know I don't want to watch this.

We continue to make our way down the hall—stopping briefly as I watch a woman beautifully bound in ropes suspended from the ceiling. We also pass a woman with two men on their knees for her—but it's the woman in a room alone who draws my attention. She's sitting on a chair a few feet from the window with her legs draped over the arms, putting her on full display for everyone in the hall. She has a hot-pink toy between her legs that is both in her and resting on her clit.

"She's alone?" I inquisitively whisper to Finn.

"Not entirely," he smirks, gesturing toward the couple beside us. They are taking turns, sliding their fingers over a screen as they stare at the woman before them. It takes me a minute of watching, seeing the woman react in response to the couple's thumbs sliding over the screen, to realize that they are controlling the toy inside her. "She's getting off from letting strangers control her pleasure."

Resting with my back against Finn's chest, we watch the couple swipe the device up to high. The woman writhes in the chair, her hips grinding into the cushion as she struggles through her pleasure. Gripping her knees to keep her thighs spread, her eyes lock on mine through the sheet of glass. Unable to break our stare, I watch her unfurl as my heart begins to race and a fluttering ache builds between my own thighs.

"And she fucking loves being watched," Finn whispers as his lips dust along my neck. His hands roam over me, lightly cupping my breast as the woman's eyes bore into mine. Arousal trickles down my thigh, and I lean into Finn, chewing at my lower lip as she comes again. "And judging by the scent of you, you fucking love watching her."

I do.

More than I ever could have imagined. I'm so turned on right now, I'd probably come if Finn so much as touched me.

"This way," Finn commands, forcing me to break my stare as he drags me away from the window. "There's another room I want to show you."

We pass a few occupied rooms, stopping at a brightly lit section of the hallway with a large mirror the same size as the windows lining the other rooms. Curious, I cup my eyes and press my face to it, trying to see what's inside. "I can't see anything."

"That's the point," Finn swipes a keycard to open the door. Reaching through the threshold, he flips a switch, and a red light turns on above the mirror. The light draws the attention of a number of other guests as he extends his hand and pulls me into him the moment I accept it. Dragging me into the room and shutting the door, he asks, "Do you want see if you like being watched as much as you like watching, *piscín*?"

CHAPTER THIRTY-SEVEN
CATLIN

When I step further into the room, I startle upon seeing faces pressed tightly to the window. Turning toward Finn, he quickly reads the hesitant look on my face. "It's a one-way mirror, piscín."

"So, *I* can see *them*"—I wave my hand before the glass, noting that it doesn't garner a single reaction from the faces pressed to it—"but *they* can't see *me*."

Closing the distance between us, Finn asks, "Could you see inside when you looked through it?" Not a thing. I lightly shake my head, as Finn sweeps my hair over my shoulder to reveal the zipper of my dress. He lowers it an inch before imparting, "If you aren't okay with this, we don't have to."

My heart pounds, and nervous energy courses through me as I think about the woman down the hall. She came countless times from the toy and the couple, but they were nothing compared to how she had completely exploded with bliss as I watched her. Unable to deny my curiosity, I glance over my shoulder at Finn and try to hide my hesitation when I brat, "Did I ask to go to church?"

A devilish smirk pulls at the corner of his mouth as he drags the zipper down the length of my spine. "No. No, you did not," he replies, slipping my dress from my shoulders and letting the soft fabric flutter down my body. Standing before the window wearing nothing but my strappy heels, I stare into the sea of faces before me.

When I turn around, I find Finn tossing his shirt to the floor as he undoes his pants. Standing behind me, he snakes his arms around me and slides his hands down my stomach. His fingers travel through the crease of my hips and between my legs. A growl rattles in his chest as his palms rub over the slickness covering my upper thighs, and his voice is gravelly. "I love how fucking wet my good girl gets when she's being naughty."

Kissing along my neck, he pulls gently at my thighs, urging me to widen my stance. He toys with my nipples, rolling them between his fingers until I'm wound so tightly that I'm ready to explode. "Does *mo piscín* need me to make good on my promise?" He chuckles as I grind against his hard length and writhe against him.

"Please," I beg, desperately needing him inside me.

Goosebumps of excitement prickle my skin as he dusts his fingertips from my shoulders to my wrists. Grabbing my hands, he lifts them and roughly slams them against the glass before me, startling the people trying desperately to watch from the other side.

"Eyes on them. Watch their faces," Finn commands as he pushes his pants down his thighs and presses his length to my entrance. I've taken precautions to be safe—with Layla's help—but Finn's next words still catch me off-guard. "See how fucking excited they are to watch me finally take you bare."

Finn sinks the entirety of his shaft into me, and a breathy grunt billows from my lungs as he suddenly stretches me. Pressing against the glass, I arch my back and push into him, needing him to take me like he promised. But Finn knows exactly what I need; he grips my hips and slams into me again, groaning, "Fuck, Cat. Feeling every bit of your cunt wrapped around me is fucking heaven."

My fingertips try to find purchase into the pane of glass as he takes me hard and fast, demanding that I come for him. The wall of faces stares at me, watching me hurdle toward my release. I can't believe how much I enjoy fantasizing that they are actually watching what Finn does to me. That they're watching how good he makes me feel.

"Come for me," Finn instructs, deepening his rough thrusts and raking his nails along my spine. "Come for *them*. Show them how hard I pray at your altar as I worship your sweet, dripping pussy."

My body does exactly as he commands, and I slip off the edge I was teetering on. Screams of pleasure fall over my lips, and the men and women watching react. It feels like they're actually watching me come undone. Finn rubs vigorously at my clit as he slams into me from behind, and my orgasm doesn't stop. The wave of pleasure comes again and again as everyone stares at me in awe. I come until my thighs are trembling and I can barely stand.

"One more for me," Finn grunts the command. "One more as I fill you, mark every inch of your sweet heaven with my cum, finally claiming it as mine."

Struggling to stand on my quivering legs, I clench around Finn as he grows more rigid inside me. He slams into me with a roar, and I cry out in pleasure, coming again as he unloads his release.

Finn's hips still with him buried deep inside of me, and he breathlessly slumps against my sweat-covered back. Catching his breath, his kisses over my salty skin as he whispers, "You're mine, *piscín*."

A few moments later, he pulls himself from me and tucks himself back into his pants before retrieving my panties from his pocket. Dropping to his knees, he carefully slips them over my heels, drags them up my legs, and pulls them over my hips. "Mine," he growls, running his fingers over the lacy fabric as he stares into my eyes. "You're the first woman I've ever truly marked as mine."

Finn dips his face and softly presses his lips to mine. He pulls back a breath, his words vibrating across my lips as he whispers, "And you're going to be the only one."

CHAPTER THIRTY-EIGHT

FINNIGAN

"Please. Just hear me out," Cat begs before placing her phone onto the kitchen island. Her face etched with disappointment.

"He'll come around," I try to comfort her, rubbing my hand over her back and hating how Father O'Flaherty is treating her. "It's barely been a month."

"You think?" Her voice holds so much hope that I can't bear to say anything negative.

"*Piscín*, he's been finding reasons to hate me for at least twenty years," I half-heartedly joke, trying to lighten the mood. "He just needs a little time to learn that I am absolutely amazing and how happy you are with me. He *will* come around."

Even if I have to force him.

"Are you sure you're going to be okay here today?" I hate the thought of leaving her when she's so upset.

"No, Finn," she brats. "I'm a fragile little thing, and I need you to take care of me every waking minute of the day."

Spinning her barstool, I step between her thighs and cup her face. "Don't fucking tempt me." My snarl is more of a tease than anything else.

"Go." Cat huffs, playfully pushing me away from her. "Go do mafia crap with your brothers or something."

"Mafia crap? Is that what we're calling it now?"

"It sounds better than *criminal* crap," she quips, climbing off her barstool with a smirk. Grabbing her wrist as she passes, I pull her into me and kiss her bratty lips. "Go. I will be fine. I'm meeting up with Layla and we're heading over to Quinn's this after-noon," she firmly demands while cupping my face.

"Don't go anywh—"

She interrupts with a heavy sigh and mocks the instructions I provide every time I'm not with her. "Don't go anywhere without Owen and William. And make sure I have my phone. The ringer needs to be on, and it must be fully charged before I leave the house. If anything seems wrong, call you immediately."

While I don't appreciate the sarcastic mockery in the slightest, I take a great deal of comfort in the fact she knows exactly what I intended to tell her. Even more in the knowledge she will follow her rules to a T.

It's a lot.

I didn't think much of it when Tris and Dec brought women into our family, but Layla, Quinn, and now Cat have made a substantial sacrifice to be in our lives. As if the worry about *our* safety every time we walk out the door isn't enough, we guard them like Fort fucking Knox to ensure they don't come to any harm for the sins we commit.

"I fucking love you, *piscín*." I kiss her once more before heading toward the door. "Be safe."

"You too, *mo ghrá.*"

Fuck, do I ever love when she calls me that.

When I step into the hall and close the door to the apartment, I find Owen ready to watch over her while I can't. "Protect her at all costs." There's none of my signature joviality in my instructions.

"With my life, sir," Owen responds.

He better.

It's in his best interest to die protecting her; death would be better than what I would do to him if anything were to happen to her.

After assuring Cat's helmet is firmly fastened to the bike so that I can safely pick her up later, I pull mine on. Climbing onto the bike, I gun the ignition and pull from the garage. We've had an influx of applications to Club Triskelion lately, leaving us with a lot of new members to vet this afternoon. Which is why I leisurely weave through traffic as I make my way to meet up with my brothers.

I park in the valet at the club since it won't be used for patrons for several more hours. Conor arrives just after me, parking the Tahoe so close to my bike that I'm certain he's going to tap my rear tire as I dismount.

"Just the brother I wanted to see," Conor chirps, climbing from the SUV. He sighs as he walks toward me with a shit-eating grin on his face. "You would not believe the fucking dream I had."

"You seriously need to get fucking laid so you stop telling me about Cat starring in your wet dreams," I snark, pulling open the front door to the club.

"Who said I had a hot fucking dream and wanked to Cat?" Conor smirks, drawing Declan, Liam, and Tristan's attention as they sit at the bar, shuffling through paperwork.

"We need to find you a woman." Tristan sighs with annoyance. "Maybe then you'll stop fantasizing about ours."

"Better make it two... Maybe three, because fuck, was it ever a good dream."

"You can't be serious." Declan's face reddens with something that looks a lot like jealousy.

"The four of you need to imagine the three of them naked." He pauses for a moment and slides onto a barstool beside an annoyed Declan. "Now, imagine them thoroughly enjoying one another."

As much as I would never share Cat—with my brothers or my sisters-in-law—I cannot deny the way my cock twitches when I briefly picture her with Layla and Quinn.

They're all fucking gorgeous; it would be hot as sin.

"Yeah." Liam clears his throat. "I would totally fucking wank watching that."

"New rule," Declan gruffly declares. "The lot of you no longer talk about wanking to or fucking my wife."

"I just want it on record that I haven't wanked to thoughts of your wife in a couple of months," I share, trying very hard not to sound too smug.

Declan huffs before shoving from his seat and grabbing a bottle of Tullamore Dew from behind the bar. "Fuck the lot of you."

CHAPTER THIRTY-NINE
CATLIN

As I'm sitting in the backseat of a blacked-out Suburban as Owen drives me to Layla's place, I pull my phone from my purse and shoot her a text.

> Owen said we'll be there in about 5 minutes

LAYLA

> I'm ready, waiting in the lobby, and I just confirmed that everything is all set

> Fantastic! Finn is going to die.

> Girl, I hope you've been drinking your water because that man is going to shit bricks.

> And then he's going to fucking ruin you.

I snort at her message, drawing Owen's attention. "You okay, ma'am?"

For now...

"Fine." I chuckle as he pulls to the curb at the front of Layla's building. "And please, would you please call me Catlin?"

"Sorry, ma'am." He glances into the rearview mirror to make eye contact with me, and he shakes his head as Layla's bodyguard opens the rear passenger door for her to slip into the backseat. After closing the door, he takes the empty seat up front to come with us.

Layla gives me a tight squeeze, introduces me to Grady —who also calls me ma'am—and provides Owen with the address of our destination.

"I still can't believe you're doing this!" Layla exclaims as we make the short drive to Hell's Kitchen.

She isn't the only one.

"He's determined to mark every inch of me. I'm just helping him out," I jest. A few minutes later, we pull up to the shop. Owen opens my door for me, another of Finn's rules about safety. Walking to the door of the shop, I squeeze Layla's hand. "I really appreciate you coming with me and being my emotional-support person when I probably cry."

As we step inside, I clutch her hand even tighter. I'm surprised to find the shop isn't quite as intimidating as I expected. Plants and leather couches line the wall to my left, and it's almost cozy. The rear wall has small cubbies with a chair similar to the ones at the dentist's office. The walls of each are adorned with various art from the artist's portfolio. To my right is a large reception desk with a man sitting behind it covered in more ink than Finn. *I didn't think that was possible.* I startle when he shouts, "Fresh meat!"

"Be nice, Jimmy," Jillian reprimands him as she walks toward the desk. "I don't appreciate you talking to my clients like that—"

"This sweet little virgin-skinned piece of ass is *your* client?" He scoffs.

"Yes"—she nods—"And her boyfriend most definitely won't appreciate you talking about her like that."

"Is that so, little one?" he asks as his eyes rake over my body. "Who's your big scary boyfriend?"

"Finnigan Evans," I answer, watching his entire demeanor immediately change. The reaction those two words have on men never ceases to amaze me. I know Finn has a different side to him—*a bad one*—but the fear the kind-hearted man I love invokes in others continues to baffle me.

His eyes suddenly meet mine instead of my breasts when he talks, and he quickly stammers through an apology. "I was just kidding around. Do you need a bottle of water or anything?"

Jillian leads me to the back of the shop, but we go to a private room instead of a cubby. She gestures for me to take a seat in the black leather chair as she grabs a stool for Layla to sit beside me. She wheels up beside me on a second one. "You look nervous, sweetie. Are you sure you want to do this?"

"I am. To both," I answer. "Your work on Finn is amazing—"

"And she's seen all of it. A lot," Layla jests, helping to ease my nerves.

"If he trusts you, so do I."

"This will be fast," Jillian informs me. "But you picked a tender spot for your first one, so while I am very light-handed, I can't promise it won't hurt."

"That's what she has me for." Layla comfortingly squeezes my right hand as Jillian preps my skin.

The needle burns across my skin for an eternity—or ten minutes—before Jillian announces, "All done."

"It's so good," Layla croons as Jillian cleans my tender skin and hands me a mirror to look at her work. Layla's right. *It's perfect.*

Finn's name runs along the length of my left collar-bone in his handwriting, permanently marking me as his.

Finn is going to love it!

Layla graciously pays my tab—so Finn doesn't get a notification of my purchase—and sends a quick text to Tristan, begging him to keep my secret. The phone promptly dings in her hand, and she passes it to me to read the message. "You owe me one because this secret comes at a heavy cost."

"Because I'm sure you will absolutely hate every minute of that." I giggle. "But we should probably get over to Quinn's while you can still sit."

During rush hour, the traffic is abhorrent, and it takes us a little over an hour to make the normally thirty-minute drive to New Rochelle.

"Show me," Quinn blurts the moment we let ourselves through the front door as she tries to push her *very* pregnant body from the couch. Crossing the room to meet her, I undo the buttons of my shirt to show her Finn's name amidst my still-reddened skin. "It's beau-tiful. He's absolutely going to love it!" she exclaims.

I'm about to thank her when she grimaces and reaches for her stomach. Gently, she rubs over her swollen belly, groaning, "They're running out of room in there. They've been acting up all afternoon."

Water gushes from beneath her sundress, and her face drops when she looks down to the puddle she's now standing in.

"Pretty sure they aren't going to be fighting for much longer," Layla quips before running out the front door to let Owen, Grady, and Rory know we're leaving.

"Fi?" I call to her where she's coloring at the kitchen table as I pull my phone from my purse to send a quick text to Finn. "Baby, you need to grab your shoes. You're about to become a big sister."

CHAPTER FORTY
FINNIGAN

This afternoon of tedious paperwork has practically bored me to tears. Club Triskelion is more than profitable enough for the five of us to go legit, but I fucking love the—*as Cat so eloquently puts it*—mafia crap. I enjoy breaking kneecaps and getting shot at way too much for *this* to ever be all there is.

My phone buzzes on the bar before me, and I lift it to find a text from an unknown number.

UNKNOWN

Hey, Finnie. I've got something for you.

Fuck, I hate that nickname.

I deleted all the contact details of any women I was hooking up with before Cat, but only one ever called me that horrible nickname.

> Sorry, Mandy. I'm not interested.

> Apparently the rumors are true because you've never turned down my booty calls before.

> I also wasn't texting about my pussy.

> That guy you were looking for a few months ago, are you still looking for him?

> The Russian?

> Yeah. He's fucking one of my waitresses, and she keeps bragging about him coming to pick her up at the end of her shift.

Fuck, yes!

"Who wants to go hit something with me?" I blurt, dropping my phone onto the bar top.

Conor's eyes light up, and he jumps out of his seat. "Yes. Please! Anything but more of these fake Dom applications."

"The Pakhan is going to be at The Onyx in a few hours," I inform them as my phone buzzes again. Expecting it to be another text from Mandy, I ignore it before providing my brothers with the scant details she had given me. It vibrates against the wooden bar again, and I glance down to see two missed messages from Cat.

CATLIN

QUINN IS HAVING HER BABIES!

We are on our way to New Rochelle Memorial.

On our way.

"Change of plan." I slide from the barstool and shove the phone into the front pocket of my pants. "Quinn is in labor. The girls are all on their way to the hospital."

"Fuck," Declan barks, quickly grabbing his phone and keys. "It'll take forever to get there this time of the day."

"I've got the bike," I tell him, thankful I'm prepared as always with a spare helmet on my bike. "I can get you to New Rochelle Memorial in twenty minutes."

"We'll meet you there," Tristan chimes as we rush to the door.

It doesn't take us long to reach my bike parked out front. I throw Cat's helmet at Declan and climb onto the bike. Turning over the engine, Declan is about to climb on when he pauses. Staring at the seat behind me, he asks, "Finn. Is that cum? Please tell me it's not cum."

"On my bike?" I glance over my shoulder at the stain on the seat and lie, "No. It's not cum."

Declan grabs my shoulder and hesitantly climbs onto the bike. I rev the engine as he fists the side of my shirt, letting the loud grumble of the bike quiet before I inform him, "It's definitely fucking cum."

Not giving him a chance to respond, my tires squeal against the pavement, and I laugh as we pull from the valet and into traffic. Knowing how fucking pissed he is as we weave through the slow moving cars is worth every fucking fist I take to the kidney on the journey. Pulling up to the entrance of the hospital, he shouts as the roar of the engine quiets, "You're a fucking twat, Finn. Now I have to burn these fucking trousers."

"Stop fucking fighting with me and go to your wife." I smirk beneath my helmet. After finding a space to park my bike, I make my way inside and up to Labor and Delivery to find Cat sitting with my peanut on her lap. Owen is sitting a few chairs away, keeping an eye on them both.

"*Uncail* Finn," Fiona excitedly shouts. "I'm gonna be a big sister."

"You sure are!" I croon, giving each of them a kiss on the forehead before I take the empty seat beside the two of them. "Where's Layla?"

"She went downstairs with Grady and Rory to grab some coffee," Cat informs me.

"When are you going to have a baby?" Fiona looks between me and Cat.

Thanks, peanut...

At a loss for words for the first time in my life, I stare at Cat in silence. I absolutely adore my niece, but fatherhood had never crossed my mind. The women who passed through my bed were a fleeting good time and definitely not mother material. Cat is neither of those. She's unbelievably nurturing and sweet, amazing with Fiona, and the very last woman to ever grace my bed.

Cat gazes back at me, and I'm relieved to see her reflecting what I can only imagine is the same deer-in-the-headlights look spread across my face. Her eyes focus on my reaction as she answers Fiona, "Not for a long time, baby."

"How come?"

"Well…" Cat struggles to find an explanation Fiona will understand. "I'm still going to school."

Trying to quell her curiosity, I add, "We also haven't known each other that long."

"Yeah, but you're gonna marry her," Fiona chirps. "So you should just have a bunch of pretty babies, too."

Pulling Fiona into my lap, I tickle her, huff, and whisper, "That was supposed to be a secret."

"Not a very good one," Cat jests. While I may not have outright asked her to be my wife—*yet*—she knows that she's mine for the rest of my life. And all of eternity.

We sit in the waiting room for hours, joined by Layla and eventually the rest of my brothers. All of us doing our best to keep a quickly tiring Fiona occupied. A little shy of midnight, Declan steps into the waiting room with a tired yet elated look on his face. "They're here."

"Only three visitors at a time," a nurse announces when we all rise from our seats in near unison.

Declan glances at all of us and then back at her. "Unless you want them to beat the piss out of each other over who gets to go first, you're going to want to let them all in."

Carrying Fiona and holding Cat's hand, I follow my brothers down the hall to Quinn's room. While she's clearly exhausted, she looks absolutely radiant, lying in the hospital bed with a baby resting in each of her arms. "And this crazy lot is your family," she coos as she stares down at them before lifting her attention to all of us. "Meet Rory and Kira."

"I make a few jokes about whacking off to your wife and you beat the piss out of me." I nudge Declan. "But she names her baby after the man attached to her when you aren't around and you don't even bat an eye."

Rolling her eyes, Quinn says, "I named them after the man who nearly died to save my life and the woman who did."

With Finn following behind us on his bike, Owen and Rory bring me and Fiona back to her house. We offered to watch over her for the night so Declan could stay at the hospital with Quinn. I expected it to be a very late night of her excitedly babbling about her new siblings, but the second her little head hits the pillow, she's out cold.

Making my way downstairs, I find Finn sitting on the patio. He's enjoying a glass of whiskey beside the firepit. A broad smile spreads across his face when he sees me through the glass as I cross the room to join him.

It's unseasonably chillier than expected, and goose-bumps prickle over my arms when I step onto the patio. When I take a seat on his lap, Finn pulls me into him and kisses me, his lips tasting of woodsy spice. I nuzzle against his chest and enjoy the warmth coming from him and the fire as he holds me under the stars.

"She wasn't wrong." Finn presses his lips to my forehead. "I am going to make you my wife."

"Finn…" My voice cracks as his name falls from my lips.

"I'll give you a big, elaborate proposal if you want one, but I've promised my life—and every lifetime after— to you more times than I could count. And I mean it more with every breath I spend with you. An eternity wouldn't be long enough with you, *piscín*."

Shifting my weight and sitting up on his lap, Finn's eyes follow my fingers as I slowly undo the buttons of my shirt. "I want to be your wife, and I want you to claim me as yours before God. But I don't need those things to know how you feel about me."

My shirt is open, a slit of skin poking between the two pieces of fabric draped over my breasts as I grab Finn's shirt at his shoulders and pull it over his head. Haphazardly, I toss it to the patio and place my hand over the black cat tattooed over his heart. "I know that you're mine, Finnigan."

Slipping my shirt from my shoulders, his eyes fall to the fresh ink on my collarbone as I whisper, "And I am yours forever."

Finn pulls my shirt down my arms before pressing his lips to the tender skin. He tosses it beside his on the pavers at his feet and undoes the clasp of my bra, quickly ridding me of it and freeing my breasts. The chilly air nips at my skin and my nipples grow hard as Finn's lips trail up my neck. Kissing and nipping at my skin, Finn gravelly whispers, "I've already claimed you as mine on God's altar, but I'll happily do it again under his heaven."

Lifting me from his lap, Finn licks and sucks at my tight nipples as he removes my shorts and panties. He pulls me back onto his lap so that I'm straddling him. His large hands roughly palm my butt as he grinds me over the growing length pressing into me in his pants. Gripping his shoulders, I swirl my hips, trying to work myself to the edge.

"Do you need my cock?" he taunts, raking his finger-tips down my back.

My chest heaving and unable to get myself there, I nod. "Please."

"Tell me," he demands, firmly gripping my hips and roughly grinding me over his bulging zipper. His words grow breathy and needy. "Tell me you need my cock. That you want me in your tight little pussy. Tell me how you want to be ruined as I come inside you."

"Please, Finn," I beg again.

"Tell me, *piscín*."

Unable to take the ache between my thighs, I groan, "I need you... I need you inside me."

As he lifts us both from the chair, my legs wrap around Finn's waist, and he carries me across the patio. Finn presses me against the house, and I squeal as the bare skin of my back presses against the cold sheet of glass. He sloppily claims my mouth, fumbling beneath me to undo his pants. He slips part of his tip inside me, and I moan with need when he stills. Firmly holding my thighs, he prevents me from taking more of him.

"You want to be claimed before God?" He roughly pulls me over his length until he bottoms out inside of me. "I'm going to fuck you so hard he'll hear you screaming his name as you come."

My back is pinned to the glass as Finn aggressively slams the entirety of himself into me with every blissfully painful drive. My chest heaves against him, and I pant through his vigorous thrusts. Hovering on the edge, my nails dig into his shoulders.

"Come. For. Me," Finn grunts between thrusts. Burying himself deep, he grinds his hips against my entrance. "Which god will you be screaming for when you come?"

Unable to answer through my labored breaths, my hips grind against him with his length buried inside me.

"Him?" Finn pulls out and slams into me again. "Or me?"

"Finn!" I breathlessly scream as the orgasm building at my center fires through every nerve in my body, completely shattering me.

"Good girl," Finn groans against my neck as he picks up his pace. Every inch of my body is on fire as he continues to drive into me, not letting me come down from my orgasm before demanding another from me. "Tell him again, *piscín*. Scream into his heavens and let him know who your god really is."

My back arches from the glass, and I claw at Finn and scream his name as I come again. I writhe over him as I clench around him, wanting more and needing him to stop in equal measure.

Finn squeezes my thighs bruisingly hard, driving into me with such force that my toes curl. He thrusts again, spilling himself into me as he roars, "Fuck! Cat!"

CHAPTER FORTY-TWO
CATLIN

A COUPLE OF DAYS LATER

QUINN

Have you tried to talk to your uncle lately?

Daily.

He won't take my calls.

That's what I thought.

Why?

I reached out about setting up the baptism for Rory and Kira. He politely requested that I contact Saint Bernadette's.

That maybe they'd be a better fit for our family

I'm sorry

I haven't been to mass since Uncle Sean forced me out of his life, but Quinn has let me know a few times that he's been cordial when she's approached him after mass. *Cordial, not friendly.*

> I'll get him to reconsider

"Please don't hang up," I blurt when Uncle Sean answers the church phone, promptly hearing the click of his dropping it into the receiver. When I redial his number, I'm not surprised that it goes to voicemail.

He can't ignore me if I'm standing in front of him.

I send a quick text to Owen and William before changing my clothes.

> Please get the car ready. I need to go somewhere.

WILLIAM
> Yes, ma'am.

> I'll be ready in about ten minutes.

OWEN
> I'll be outside your door in five.

I rummage through the closet in the master bedroom for a shirt that will cover the tattoo below my shoulder. Pulling a light cardigan over my tank top, I also change from my denim shorts to a pair of jeans.

As promised, Owen is ready and waiting when I step from the hallway into the apartment. "Where are we heading in such a rush, ma'am?"

"Church. Our Lady of Grace," I inform him as we ride the elevator down to the garage where William is waiting with the Suburban. On the short drive to the church, I try a few times to call Finn to tell him where I'm going, but the call rings through to his voicemail each time.

"Can you message Finn and let him know where we are?" I ask as William flips on his hazard lights and stops before the church.

"As soon as I park, ma'am," he responds. Owen slides from the SUV and opens my door to escort me into the church. William turns off the hazard lights and pulls away from the curb as Owen lags behind me, making my way up the steps.

"Please head inside," Owen urges, his eyes following a black SUV trailing closely behind William.

Suddenly, they ram into the back of our Suburban, prompting William to stop. The moment he steps from the Suburban to survey the damage, two loud pops echo down the street, and my heart stops. A shrill scream rises from my lungs as I watch William crumple to the pavement. In shock, I can't comprehend what's happening and what danger I'm in.

"Inside!" Owen shouts as he races up the steps to close the distance between us. Wrapping his arm around me when he reaches me, he pulls me into him and shrouds me with his body as he drags me up the steps. He shoves me through the door of the church and expels a pained grunt as he stumbles in behind me. Forcing himself to his feet, he grabs at his back and unconvincingly winces. "I'm fine, ma'am. We have to get you inside."

A deafening bang echoes through the church, and my blood runs cold as I watch Owen's head blow across the door. "No, you aren't." A gruff Russian accent startles me from the threshold of the narthex as I slap my hand over my mouth to hold back my need to both vomit and scream.

Spinning around, I find a gun pointed at my face. Ink-covered hands are wrapped around it. My eyes continue down the heavily tattooed arms to find a massive man with a tinge of gray in his hair. His dark eyes meet mine, and he gruffs, "And neither are you."

My phone rings in my purse as he grabs my arm and roughly pulls me through the narthex, where other men and Uncle Sean are waiting.

"Catlin," Uncle Sean painfully cries as I'm shoved into the nave. His bloody face is dripping over his shirt, and his left eye has swollen almost completely shut.

"You should've just called her. It would've saved you a lot of pain." The Russian snarls at Uncle Sean as he wraps his arm around my throat. Tightening his grip, he pulls me into him with my back against his chest. He runs the cold barrel of his gun along my jaw, forcing me to turn my face toward him. As I stare into his cold, dark eyes, he continues moving the gun down my neck and around the swell of my breast. His touch runs chills down my spine, but his words turn my blood into ice. "I've been dreaming about getting my hands on you."

My phone rings again, and the Russian rips my purse from hand and tosses it to one of the other men. He rifles through my bag, pulls out my phone, and holds the screen toward the man holding me. "It's Finnigan."

"Send it to voicemail," the Russian commands, still traversing his gun down my body. When it rests between my thighs, he whispers, "I didn't get my chance with the bar whore, but I fully intend to make up for that with you. And when I'm done fucking ruining you, I'll let my boys have a turn. When they're done, we'll call your little boyfriend to see what we've done to you before we kill him."

Owen's phone rings, echoing from the vestibule, and I struggle to find the courage to spit, "That's Finn, making sure I got here okay."

"The idiotic man who fucked anything with two legs and cunt is fucking obsessed with you, huh?" he taunts, squeezing my throat harder as he continues to rub his gun between my thighs. Bile rises higher in my throat with every word that passes over his lips. "That little pussy of yours must be something spectacular."

My phone rings again, and the Russian gestures at the man holding it. As he walks closer, the Russian takes his gun from my thighs and rams it against my cheek, warning, "I'll blow your fucking pretty face across this church if you do anything stupid."

CHAPTER FORTY-THREE
FINNIGAN

Sitting in front of the main stage of The Onyx with Conor, I sip my glass of whiskey as I repeatedly turn down offers for lap dances and trips to the Champagne Room. Not only is it not what I'm here for, I'm also not interested. The only woman I want rubbing her tits in my face and grinding—*preferably pantyless*—over my lap is Catlin.

Conor, on the other hand, is currently wearing the perfume and glitter of about ten different strippers and is impatiently waiting for the pretty little brunette on stage to slide onto his lap.

Her ass overtly swaying with every step, Mandy saunters over to the two of us with a tray of drinks. "Sorry, Finnie." She helps herself to my thigh and takes a seat as she places our drinks on the small table between me and Conor. "But you haven't let a woman touch you since the two of you got here, and considering you've fucked half of them, you look suspicious as fuck."

"Told you," Conor chimes as the petite brunette climbs from the stage and slides over his thighs. "I'm just blending."

Knowing they're both right, I place my hand on the small of Mandy's back and uncomfortably rub it over her hip as she sits on my thigh.

"Fuck, Finnie," she snarks. "Could you be any more awkward? Most married guys come in here so hungry for pussy they can't keep their hands off the talent."

"Trust me, that man gets more pussy now than he did when he was single." Conor laughs into the perky tits spilling against his face. "But fuck, if I had a girl who was as fucking hot as his, I'd be inside her all the time, too."

"For fuck's sake, Conor," I huff as the girl on his lap whispers something into his ear. A devilish smirk spreads across his face as she slides from his lap.

"Keep it in your pants, big boy," Mandy teases. "Because she's the girl. The one dating the Russian."

"Oh, fuck!" Conor huffs. "You couldn't have shared that before she offered to let me fuck her?"

"It's a revenge fuck," she informs him. "Her boyfriend blew her off tonight, so now she wants to fuck some stranger to piss him off."

"Cat isn't expecting me until nine," I inform him, glancing at my watch. "I've got at least five minutes before we need to go. That should be more than enough time for you to take her for a ride at least twice."

"Fuck, if that's all it takes you, no wonder Cat's always eyeing me up," he teases, just to piss me off. *And it works.* "Besides, I'd rather go home and wank off to Cat so I can call you and tell you all about it."

"Good plan," Mandy chimes. "Because I'm pretty sure any men stupid enough to stick his cock in her will be dead by the morning."

"I will beat the ever-loving piss out of you if you so much as *think* about wanking to Cat when I take you home," I snarl as we walk toward the exit.

"Bring it on, Finn," he smirks. "Because I'm totally thinking about it."

Fuck, no wonder Declan used to beat my ass all the time.

When we step from the club, my phone immediately dings and lights up with three missed calls from Catlin. "Fuck. I forgot that place has no reception."

The phone rings through to her voicemail when I try to call her back. Swiping through my contacts, I try William and am met with his voicemail. This time, I dial Cat again, my heart racing, and I bark at Conor, "Get in the fucking truck."

"Fuck, bro. Of all people, Cat isn't going to lose her shit because you're a few minutes late.

"Get in the fucking truck," I shout. "Something isn't right."

Turning over the engine to the Bronco, the Bluetooth kicks on as I'm sent to voicemail again, "Hey, you've reached Catlin. Leave me a message and I'll—"

"Try Owen," I roar at Conor, shoving my phone at him as we peel from the parking lot. It goes to voicemail as well, so I demand, "The apartment."

It rings a handful of times before Conor ends the call. My fingers grip the steering wheel until my knuckles are white, and I race toward the apartment where I had left her.

"I'll try her again," Conor insists, swiping through my phone.

It rings twice, and she finally answers, "Hey, sweetie."

My heart is still racing. Something isn't right. "Are you okay?"

"I'm fine." Her answer is curt. No woman is ever okay when they say they're fine.

"You didn't answer my ca—"

She interrupts and reiterates herself, "I said I'm fine."

"Where is Owen?" I press, unease coursing through me. "Or William?"

"Finn, stop," she replies. "I told you I was going to **church**."

"I'm sorry, kitten," I feign an apology and stomp on the accelerator.

Her tone softens slightly, and her voice cracks when she says, "I'll call you when I'm on my way home."

The call abruptly ends, and Conor shifts in the passenger seat. "What the hell, Finn? She's at church with Father O'Flaherty. She's fine."

"She's not." I shake my head and veer through traffic at grossly unsafe speeds. "She has never called me 'sweetie,' and she said she's at church."

Conor stares at me in complete confusion for a moment. "I'm so fucking lost right now."

"*Church*," I emphasize the word. "It's her safeword. She told me to stop and used her safeword. She's in fucking trouble."

"Fuck!" Conor exclaims, swiping through my phone. "I'll call the others."

"There isn't time." I pull down the block that runs along the convent. "Because I'm not fucking waiting."

CHAPTER FORTY-FOUR
CATLIN

"That little shit is fucking obsessed with you." The Russian darkly chuckles. "And I can't fucking wait to find out why."

He didn't shoot me, but what I think he has planned might be worse than death.

Keeping calm throughout the call with Finn, tears trickle down my face as they end the call. My heart breaks, worrying that I'll never see him again and hoping desperately that he knows I was screaming for him to come and help me.

Please know I'm not just at church. Please save me.

"That's a good girl," the Russian croons, further tightening his already painful grip around my throat. Turning me to face him, he eyes the salty droplets trickling down my face, and the depths of his eyes turn soulless. He swipes his fingers over my wet skin and whispers, "Your tears are fucking beautiful."

I try to hold them back, not wanting to give him the satisfaction of affecting me, but my body betrays me. Tears flow uncontrollably from my eyes, streaming down my face and dripping from my chin as I sob.

"And they taste even better," the Russian groans with disgusting delight as he licks the underside of my chin and up my cheek. Desperately, I grip his wrist with both hands and try to pull him from me as I struggle to breathe. He cleans my other cheek with his tongue. "I can't help but wonder if all of you tastes this good..."

Turning me away from him again, he uses his grip on my neck to pin my back against his chest. His gun returns between my thighs, and I tremble in fear as he firmly rubs it against me through my jeans. Adjusting his hold on the butt of it, he pulls at the top of my jeans, trying to undo the button. As he glances down, trying to find my zipper, he asks, "Is the rest of you as fucking soaked as your beautiful face?"

Clenching my jaw, I exhale ragged breaths as he takes his time lowering my zipper.

"Who cares if she's fucking wet?" one of the guys standing near Uncle Sean interjects as he overtly grabs his crotch. "She'll take all our fucking cocks regardless."

The Russian holding me quickly lifts his gun, and I barely hear the shot before the man talking has a hole in the center of his forehead. I startle and bite my tongue to keep myself from screaming.

"I care." The warm words blow against the shell of my ear. "I want you to know how much your body fucking loves what I'm doing to it. Your body betraying you as your pussy drips, and you repeatedly come around my cock; hating yourself for enjoying how fucking good it feels."

He loosens his tight hold on my throat, and my lungs burn as I suck in a deep breath. Sliding the gun up my stomach, he wraps his arm around my neck. His free hand drags roughly along the side of my body, and he whispers, "Be a good girl and cry for me."

His fingertips dip beneath the waistband of my panties, and Uncle Sean shouts, "Stop!"

The Russian sighs as he pulls his fingers out of my panties. "Are you going to be like this all fucking night? I like my women screaming, not their fucking families."

"He's just fucking jealous," a man with a wine stain on his cheek snarks.

"Is that it, Father?" The Russian walks toward Uncle Sean, dragging me with him. "Are you fucking jealous?"

Using the gun to tip my face up to him, the Russian's eyes bore through me. "Did you never spread those curvy thighs of yours for your uncle?"

"You're disgusting," I spit, my stomach turning at the thought.

"All those years of owning her tight little ass and this tease never let you have a taste?" The Russian pushes me closer toward Uncle Sean. "I'm not letting anyone in her little cunt before me, but I bet those pouty lips of hers suck one hell of a cock."

This cannot be happening.

Where are you, Finn?

The Russian grips my shoulder so hard that I wince in pain as he pushes to me to my knees at Uncle Sean's feet. "Maybe if she sucks your stubby celibate cock, you'll shut the fuck up long enough for me to enjoy her a time a two. I'll even let you watch as I bend her over your altar."

I glance at Uncle Sean; he looks like a broken shell of the angry man who banished me from this church a couple of months ago. A tear trickles down his cheek when he looks down at me and mutters, "Just shoot me."

"Not until you shoot your load down her throat," one of the men jests, and laughter erupts through the church.

Taking advantage of their distraction, I look at Uncle Sean and mouth, 'Finn is coming.'

Hopefully, really soon.

CHAPTER FORTY-FIVE
FINNIGAN

Pulling the Bronco to the curb, I park at our spot. The little slab of concrete sidewalk where Cat fell in love with me. The place I decided beyond any doubt she was the last woman I would ever be with.

I promised her an eternity with me; a vow I will not break.

Not bothering to turn off the SUV, I slide from the driver's seat and onto the street. Reaching across to cut the engine from the passenger seat, Conor calls after me, "Fuck, Finn. They'll be here in five minutes."

"And she could be fucking dead in five minutes," I retort as a painful realization creeps into my thoughts. *I might already be too fucking late. She might already be dead.* As much as I know storming the church alone is fucking foolish, I pop the tailgate and grab my bat. Next, I lift the lid to the storage compartment and pull out a Glock, which I tuck into the waistband of my trousers.

Joining me at the back of the Bronco, Conor extends his hand. "I'm not letting you go in there alone. So, are you going to give me a fucking gun or not?"

Without looking a him, I grab a second Glock and slap it into his awaiting palm before grabbing two magazines for each of us. Closing the hatch, I cross the sidewalk to the brick wall I have scaled countless times. When I climb over the wall, Conor asks, "What the fuck are you doing?"

"How the fuck do you think I got in and out of here to see Cat all that time we were sneaking around?" I snark. "Did you think I just rang the fucking bell and asked Father O'Flaherty to let me in so I could fucking rail his niece?"

"You're a fucking dick," Conor quips, following me over the wall.

The courtyard is empty, and we quickly make our way through the garden to the rear door that leads to the altar. Slipping inside, we're met with the echoes of dark laughter.

"It isn't going to suck itself, sweetheart," a thick Russian accent sneers.

Relief washes over me—*she's still fucking alive*—as unbridled rage, like no other I've ever felt before, begins to course through my veins. Seeing red, I burst through the threshold to find the Pakhan, four men, and Father O'Flaherty at the pew in the rear of the church. *No sign of Cat.* I fire off a round, and it drops one of the Bratva standing in a pew beside the badly beaten Father. Rushing in behind me, Conor fires two shots, one grazing the man standing in the aisle.

Grunting, he reaches into the pew near Father O'Flaherty. My rage reaches boiling point when he pulls Catlin to her feet by her hair as he stands and shoves his gun under her chin, warning, "Another fucking move and this pretty little girlfriend of yours isn't going to have a face."

"It's going to be okay, *piscín*," I inform her, my eyes quickly glancing from her to the two men pointing their guns at me and Conor. "Did they hurt you?"

She timidly shakes her head, and the Pakhan presses his gun firmly into her skin. My finger flexes against the trigger of my Glock as I struggle to pull the trigger, time seemingly standing still as I grapple with whether or not to shoot the Pakhan. The fear of him getting off a round if I miss and losing Cat is the only thing stopping me.

My brothers silently filter through the vestibule and into the nave, making the decision for me. Declan presses his gun into the back of the Pakhan's skull, causing him to startle. Liam and Tristan shoot the other men.

"Always so fucking impatient." Declan chuckles at me. Reaching around the Pakhan, Declan pulls the gun from beneath Catlin's chin as he calmly instructs. "Catlin, sweetheart. Go to Finn."

A torrent of tears are streaming down her face as Cat races down the aisle toward me. The Pakhan seethes and grows redder with every stride Cat makes toward me. When she is a few pews from me, he whips his head back, connecting with Declan's face and breaks his nose. The crunch of the splintering bone carries through the church as the Pakhan raises his gun in my direction. His barrel doesn't point at me but at Cat.

Losing her would be worse than losing my life.

Unaware of the danger she's in, Cat continues to run toward me.

Shots echo through the church, each of my brothers putting a round into the Pakhan as Cat crashes into me. Enveloping her in my embrace, she falls to the floor. She sobs into my chest as I hold her. Tenderly kissing the top of her forehead, I whisper, "You're okay, *piscín*. I've got you. We'll never let anything happen to you."

When she calms, I leave her at the altar with Conor. Dragging the barrel of my bat against the hardwood floor as I walk down the aisle, I reach the Pakhan— lying in an ever-growing pool of his own blood—who is struggling to breathe. His eyes widen when I shove the barrel under his bloody chin to garner his attention.

My nostrils flare as I stare down at the dying piece of shit at my feet. Gripping the bat with both hands, I raise it above my head. "This is for touching what's mine." I bring the bat down across his chest, and he lets out a pained cry as droplets of blood on his soaked shirt fly into the air. He crumbles beneath my second blow as I crack his ribs, and I snarl, "And *that's* for what you fucking did to Quinn."

Raising the bat again, I look over my shoulder to find Cat huddled against Conor. She closes her eyes and gives a tiny nod before turning into his embrace. I swing that bat with every ounce of strength I possess, and the barrel drives through his face toward the floor. "And that's to ensure you never come for either of them ever fucking again."

With my chest heaving, I drop the bat and meet Father O'Flaherty's gaze. He glances toward the altar at Cat and back at me, instructing, "Go. Get her out of here. I'll figure out what to tell the police."

"We can't. It's Finn's birthday, and we have plans," I regretfully inform Uncle Sean, not wanting to cancel the surprise I have been planning with Tristan for Finn.

It has been a rough few weeks—with many tears and uncomfortable conversations—but Uncle Sean is slowly coming around to the fact that Finnigan isn't going anywhere. His stance on Finn clearly softening when he didn't inform the police of his—or his broth-er's—presence at the church that night. *It's like none of us were there.*

Together, we went and saw Uncle Sean briefly at the hospital as he recovered from the Bratva beating, but this is the first time he has requested to include Finn when we get together for our now weekly dinner date. I absolutely hate turning down his invitation to have us both over and don't want to miss this opportunity. "Tomorrow night? How about you come here and we'll make dinner for you?"

The phone is silent for a moment, and when he hesitantly agrees, a grin spreads across my face.

"That best not be one of my brothers making you smile that big," Finn teases when he walks into our bedroom to find me on the phone.

Silently shushing him, I return to my call. "I'll text you our address, and we'll see you tomorrow night. Anytime between five and six will be perfect."

"Who are we seeing tomorrow night?" Finn asks as I end my call and send Uncle Sean a quick text.

"Uncle Sean is coming for dinner," I inform him and share the details of our conversation before shooing him from the room so that I can finish getting ready for tonight.

Arriving at the club, we are both provided an envelope by one of the hostesses. Finn receives the same white envelope provided to all the members this evening, whereas I'm handed the lone red one from the stack. Finn curiously turns his over as we walk through the lounge and into the club, toward a table where his brothers and Layla are already enjoying a round of drinks.

While I receive a knowing glance or two, none of them says a word about Finn's birthday surprise. And knowing this family, I am still in complete shock that any of them have managed to keep this a secret for the week we've been planning it.

After taking our seats, Finn slips his card from the envelope. I open mine and discreetly pull out a lace eye mask, which I slip on as he reads.

Club Triskelion is hosting a special event tonight.
One of our couples will be partaking in a club-wide CNC scene. Guests are asked to enjoy their visit as usual but to kindly refrain from touching or impeding in the play of the masked submissive and her Dominant, who will be clearly identifiable by the red lipstick on his cheek.

Lifting his gaze from the card in his hands, Finn's eyes are full of excitement when he turns to find my lace-covered face. Leaning toward him, I place a kiss on his cheek—leaving a bright-red lip print on his skin—and whisper, "Happy Birthday, *mo ghrá*."

I push my chair from the table to stand, informing him, "I don't plan to make this easy."

Without a pause, Finn shoves his seat away from the table and pulls me into him, whispering, "Then I don't plan to be gentle."

My heart races as I stare up at him, excitement already coursing through me. "Maybe give me a sixty-second head start?" I request.

Finn slips his finger under my chin and tips my face up to his as a devilish smirk tugs at the corner of his lips. "You get thirty, so you better fucking run."

I dart from the table, immediately regretting my choice of shoes this evening, as I dart through the crowd. My heels click roughly against the black marble floors, and I try to count the seconds as I put distance between me and Finn, but my heart is pounding so loudly that I can barely think. Shrouded by the crowd, I turn and run in a different direction, hoping to prolong my chase.

"Do you really think you can outrun me?" Finn's voice booms over the crowd as he pushes through it behind me. *He can't be more than a few feet away.*

A rough hand brushes against my arm, and I squeal as I spin around—thinking I've already been caught—only to find Conor towering over me. Knowing I gave myself away, my eyes quickly scan the crowd and find Finn several feet away, hungrily staring back at me. "There you are, *piscín*. Don't run from me, and I'll think about taking it easy on you."

I push away from Conor and run between the bar tables toward the lounge, with my heart racing and Finn rushing in my direction. Struggling for traction on the slippery floor in my heels, I tip over empty chairs as I run, trying to slow him. But it's futile. Finn hurdles a chair and crashes into me, taking us both to the cold marble floor with a painful thud. Breathless screams for help billow from my lungs as he climbs over me, his hard length pressing against me as he pins me face-down to the cool tiles. Even though I'm only playing along, adrenalin rushes through every synapse in my body.

Finn reaches between us and roughly pulls my dress up my legs. Struggling beneath him, I claw at the tiles as he gravelly whispers, "I should fuck you right here and let everyone see what happens when you run from me."

My heart pounds in my throat—*and between my thighs* —and I struggle to breathe as Finn snakes his hand under the skirt of my dress and roughly pulls at my panties.

He wouldn't...

I feel the thin, lacy fabric begin to tear as he tugs a second time.

Or would he?

I throw back my head, and it crunches into his face, causing him to let out a pained grunt. It hurts like hell but catches him off-guard enough that I manage to squirm from beneath him. Clambering to my feet, I shove into the crowd as he snarls, "You're going to fucking pay for that, Catlin."

CHAPTER FORTY-SEVEN
FINNIGAN

"Well played, *piscín*," I mutter, rubbing my hand over my sore cheekbone as I push myself to my feet.

Working my way through the crowd in the direction she ran, I can practically smell her fear—*and her arousal*—as I stalk toward her.

"I know you're close," I taunt into the crowd. "I can smell that sweet fucking cunt of yours dripping down your legs."

Passing the viewing hall, I glance down it to see her pushing through couples engrossed in whatever's happening beyond the windows.

That's a dead-end, piscín.

You're mine, now.

We both shove our way down the hall, me about five feet behind my little kitten. Catlin repeatedly glances over her shoulder as she tugs at the door handles, trying to find a place to hide. She disappears through a threshold a few feet from me, and I reach the door just as she's trying to shove it shut. I slam into it with my shoulder and force my way into the room as she screams, "Please, don't!"

With a clunk, I close the door and flip the lock, pulling the string to draw the blinds on the window before stalking toward her. She retreats from me, quickly finding herself backed into a corner. Slinking closer, I gruff, "I told you that you can't run from me. I will *always* find you. And when I do, I'll remind you that you're mine. Always mine."

Pouncing, I spin her around and pin her to the wall with my body. In desperation, I hastily free my cock, and I tear her already ruined panties from her body before sinking into her soaking wet cunt. Taking her with hard, deep thrusts, I repeatedly pound her into the wall as I grunt, "You're. Mine. Now. *Piscín.*"

Her thighs tremble, and her pussy quivers around my cock as she tries to fight her release, not wanting to give me the satisfaction of making her come. Her body betrays her, and she unfurls against the wall.

"You can't deny me," I groan against the back of her neck, slowing my thrusts. "That sweet pussy of yours knows who it belongs to me. You'll always fucking come for me."

Pulling from her, I spin her around and hoist her around my waist as I sink back into the sweet perfection between her thighs. Her back slides against the wall as I drive into her, and her thighs squeeze against me. "Are you going to come for me again?"

"Yes." The soft whimper falls over her lips. "Always for you."

I keep her on the edge, enjoying the way her eyes burn with hunger as she desperately waits to come again. Pulling her over my length, she claws at my back, and I crash my lips against hers. Her tight pussy rhythmically clenches around me again, and I claim her mouth and swallow her screams as she comes around my cock.

Stepping back from the wall, I carry her to the bed and drop us both onto the mattress. The only sound in the room is our breathless gasps as I hold her against me and roll onto my back, pushing her onto her shaking knees. "Show me how much you need to be mine," I groan, firmly gripping her hips and sliding her over my cock. "Ride me until I've marked every inch of your pussy with my cum."

Catlin places her hands on my chest, swirls her hips, and slides over my length. Letting her find her rhythm, I slide my hands up her sides and cup her heaving tits. She lets out a delicious moan as I roll both of her nipples between my fingers. Her lower lip quivers as she stares down at me, looking like a fucking angel as she rides me.

She picks up her pace, and I groan as her head falls back and her nails dig into the ink of my chest. "You feel like fucking heaven," I tell her as she comes yet again.

On the edge myself, I grab her hips to help her keep up her pace. She claws at my chest as I force her to continue to ride her high. "One more for me," I beg, "One more and I'll fill that tight little hole."

"Please," she begs, on the brink of exhaustion. Her entire body quivers as she struggles through her bliss. And I'm fucking done for. Sliding my hands up her back, I pull her to my chest and hold her close as I bury myself inside of her. Filling her with every last drop of me, I growl into her ear, "Mine."

She slumps over me, completely satiated and struggling to catch her breath as the warm air blows over her lips and against my ear. I hold her on top of me as I slowly grow soft inside her, her heart slowing as it pounds against my chest. She places a soft kiss against my lips and whispers, "Happy Birthday, *mo ghrá.*"

Palming her face, I roll on top of her and kiss her until I've stolen her breath and am ready to claim her again. "This is the best fucking birthday present I've ever gotten." I slowly sink myself inside of her as a smirk pulls at the corner of my mouth. "I already can't wait to see what you get me next year."

I have been in more fights than I can count, lived through numerous gun fights with the Bratva, and thought I was going to watch as a bullet took the woman I love from me. Yet, pulling my bike to a stop in front of Our Lady of Grace this morning is the most terrifying thing I have ever done in my entire life.

Dismounting my bike, I slide off my helmet and place it on the seat as my phone buzzes in the front pocket of my jeans. When I pull it out, I find a text from Declan.

DECLAN

Don't be a fucking twat

Really?

I poured my heart out to you last night and THIS is the brotherly advice you give me this morning.

Yes.

> Don't be fucking twat!

> You know damned well you should've
> done this months ago.

I can't even argue with him because I know he's right.

Shoving my phone back into my pocket, I take my time walking up the front steps of the church as I gather my thoughts. I take a deep breath before placing my hand on the large wooden door and pushing it open.

It's been a couple of months since I've stepped foot inside these doors. After the night I rescued Catlin and killed the Pakhan, my only other visit has been for the baptism of Rory and Kira. Entering the nave, I pause at the spot where I shattered the Pakhan's skull, unable to find any evidence of what happened that night.

Continuing down the aisle, I make my way to the confessional. When I step inside, I kneel on the worn, tufted green cushion and smirk as I recall the last time I went to my knees here—with my face buried in Cat's pussy as my naughty girl dripped down my chin and came all over my tongue. Breathing in the woodsy scent of the small room, I rest my elbows on the prayer ledge and sigh. "Forgive me, Father, for I have sinned, a fucking lot."

"Finnigan Shay Evans," Father O'Flaherty admonishes me from beyond the lattice screen.

"I'm kidding, Father. Well, sort of." I laugh, knowing he probably doesn't remotely appreciate my humor. Father O'Flaherty clears his throat, he's definitely not amused with me, and prompts me to continue. "It has been far too long since my last confession."

"Tell me your sins, son," he prompts.

I ramble through my lesser sins, informing Father O'Flaherty of my vulgar mouth and my occasional excessive consumption of alcohol.

"I won't go into detail, Father, but I have indulged in carnal sins"—*a lot of fucking carnal sins*—"for which I have no remorse or guilt."

Especially not the fuck we had in the shower this morning as I got ready to head over here.

Shit.

Focus, Finn.

"While it was just and deserved, I have taken lives. Several of them."

"And do you feel remorse for having taken a soul?"

"No," I answer honestly. "They were soulless men, and I would do it again. I *will* do it again if I need to protect my family."

Father O'Flaherty lets out a heavy sigh from behind the lattice screen separating us.

"My biggest sin of all is corrupting an innocent, for which I do not have an ounce of guilt," I confess, my heart picking up and a rush of adrenaline coursing through me. "I love her more than life itself, and I want to make that commitment to her before God."

The other side of the confessional is silent.

"I want to marry her and make her my wife, but I will not do it without your permission."

The wood floor creaks on the other side of the thin wall, and the door to Father O'Flaherty's side of the confessional slams shut.

What the hell?

He's allowed to just walk out of my confession?

Quickly rising to my feet, I open my door to find Father O'Flaherty standing on the other side.

"I want to tell you no," he informs me. Walking away from me, he takes a seat in the nearest pew as he rambles, "I don't think you're good for her. You are a criminal and a relentless sinner. The lifestyle that you and your family lead clearly puts her in so much danger. In the short time you have known her, you have completely corrupted the sweet little girl I raised."

I follow him, taking the seat beside him, and mutter, "I know."

"As much as I hate to admit it," he continues, "I have never seen Catlin as happy as she is when she's with you. It is also very clear to me that you—and your family—will go through any lengths necessary to keep her safe."

"We will," I agree. "My brothers would lay down their lives for her as quickly as I would."

"I want to tell you no, Finnigan," he reiterates his stance. "But I'm going to put my faith in God. As much as it pains me to admit, in some convoluted grand plan that I'm not privy to, I believe he brought you into her life for a reason."

"Did you just say yes?" I ask, in awe that he hasn't yet condemned me to Hell or slugged me.

"Yes," he nods. "I give you my permission to marry Catlin. But, so help me, if you ever hurt her, I will denounce my cloth and send you to Hell myself."

And there it is...

He stands from the pew and gives me a fatherly pat on the shoulder. He begins to walk toward his office, and I call after him, "Father O'Flaherty? One more thing."

"You're really pushing your luck today, aren't you, Finnigan?" he snarks.

"Probably," I quip, rising to my feet. "But this one is equally as important."

CHAPTER FORTY-NINE
CATLIN

I spent my morning with Quinn and Layla, both of them doting over me and helping me get ready. Today is a day that I never thought would come. *Especially not here, like this.* How Finn managed to pull this one off will forever remain a mystery to me.

Quinn tucks the clip of my veil into my hair and spreads the sheer fabric across my back, ensuring that it's perfect. Kneeling at my feet, Layla helps me to slip on my heels before I stand. The two of them fluff the puffy tulle of my dress. I'm so grateful for the sisters that I gained. Staring at me with watery eyes, Quinn shares, "You are the most beautiful bride I've ever seen."

"You have to say that." I rapidly blink my eyes, trying to hold back my tears.

"No, I'm *supposed* to say it." She looks at me with warmth, love, and kindness. "But I definitely mean every word."

"Stop!" I exclaim. "You'll make me cry, and then Layla will have to do this makeup all over again."

"She's right," Conor croons from the doorway. "You are fucking vision; absolutely stunning."

"We'll see you downstairs." Layla smiles as she and Quinn grab their bouquets and make their way to the door. Playfully poking her finger into Conor's chest on her way out, she warns, "No funny business with her."

"No promises." He smirks, and Layla rolls her eyes as he crosses the room to me. Reaching out a hand, he takes mine and pulls me in to place a brotherly kiss on my cheek. Holding me close and winking, he shares, "It isn't too late, you know."

"Too late for what?" I ask, pretty certain I know the answer.

"It isn't too late for you to run away with me instead." He laughs. "It would crush my baby brother. But for you, I'd get over it."

"You sure know how to sweet talk a lady," I snark with a chuckle.

"Fine. You want sweet talk." He huffs, feigning an eye roll. "We can just fuck real fast before I take you downstairs."

"If you're going to say sweet things like that, how could I possibly refuse?" I tease, slipping my arm into his. "Are you okay with sloppy seconds? Because I've already been with one Evans brother this morning."

"Gross," he grumbles as we make our way downstairs. "It was Liam, wasn't it? I fucking knew he'd get to you first."

An obnoxious laugh billows from my lungs as we reach the vestibule and stand before the doors to the nave. When they open slowly, a broad smile is still spread across my face as the organist begins to play Wagner's Bridal Chorus.

"My brother is a lucky fucking man," Conor warmly shares, placing his hand over mine and resting it in the crook of his arm. Giving it a gentle squeeze, he walks me down the aisle to where Finn is patiently waiting to take me as his wife, his eyes locked on mine. With every step closing the distance between us, my heart swells; his admiration painted across his face. Reaching the altar, Conor teasingly whispers, "Last chance."

Overhearing him, Finn quietly grunts, "Really? On our wedding day?"

"I figured it was my last shot." Conor shrugs as I slap his arm. "But for some ungodly reason, she keeps saying no." He places a chaste kiss on my cheek and passes me to Finn before he takes his place on the altar beside his brothers.

"You're so beautiful," Finn whispers, squeezing my hand as I take my spot beside him.

"You are," Uncle Sean softly agrees before beginning the nuptial mass. I barely hear a word as I stare up at the man I'm going to spend the rest of my life with.

"I promise to cherish every bit of you—the good and the bad—unconditionally," I vow, slipping a ring onto Finn's finger. "That I'll spend the rest of my life showing you how much I love you."

"This life." Finn slowly slides the band down my finger. "And every life after. I will spend all of eternity burning for you, *piscín*."

"By the power vested in me by the great state of New York, I now pronounce you man and wife." Uncle Sean smiles at the two of us. "You may now kiss the bride."

Wasting no time, Finn pulls me into him, and his lips crash into mine. His fingers slide into my hair, fisting it lightly as he presses his tongue between my lips. Plundering my mouth, he moans into me with need, leaving me wanting when he quickly pulls away. I take a moment to compose myself and open my eyes, finding Uncle Sean pulling at the back of Finn's suit jacket as he snarls, "For the love of Christ, Finnigan Shay Evans. Have some respect for my church."

"Sorry, Father." Finn wipes spittle from his chin and mine. Turning back toward me, he mouths, '*I'm not sorry.*'

I snicker at his confession as he pulls me into him, and he hastily walks me back up the aisle as the recessional plays. "You're going to find out how not sorry I am the moment I get you into the back of the limo outside."

CHAPTER FIFTY

FINNIGAN

As we walk up the aisle and then race down the church steps, all I can think about is getting Catlin into the back of the awaiting limousine to finally claim her as my wife.

She slides across the seat, and I slip in beside her, immediately pushing the button to raise the partition. No one is going to see my wife in this position but me. The moment it's closed, I drop onto my knees before her and lift the many fabric layers of her gorgeous gown, laying them on her lap.

Grabbing her hips, I roughly drag her ass to the edge of the seat in one swift motion before pulling her lacy panties to the side. "Now, be a good little wife and come all over my face."

I bury my face between her thighs and lick up every delicious bit of arousal dripping from her sweet little pussy. Her sweet moans and whimpers fill the car, causing my cock to achingly rub against the zipper of my trousers. I suck her hard clit into my mouth and swirl my tongue around it until it's throbbing and she's writhing against my face. After releasing her clit, I slide two fingers into her with ease.

"My sweet wife is so fucking wet for me," I groan against her pussy as I curl my fingers inside her. I work them fast and hard, demanding that she falls off the edge she's teetering on. Needing her to come all over my face and my hand so that I can finally sink my aching cock into her.

"Finn," she pants my name and laces her fingers through my hair. She fists it so tightly that the burn radiates along my scalp as she drags my tongue *exactly* where she wants it. Holding me in place, she grinds her hips over my face and her thighs squeeze against my ears as her screams of pleasure fill the car.

"Such a good little wife," I praise, pulling my fingers from her. I suck them into my mouth and lick them clean before undoing my pants. Pausing for a moment to take in Catlin in all her beauty, I shove them down my thighs and my hard cock springs free.

"I'll be gentle next time," I promise, plunging the entirety of me into her with a single thrust. "Right now, I need to fucking mark you as my wife."

Violently slamming my lips against hers, I thrust into her with force as I claim her mouth at the same time. She whimpers into mine as I fuck her, licking and sucking the taste of herself from my tongue. Breaking our kiss, a guttural moan passes over her pouty pink lips as her back arches from the seat.

"That's a good girl. Show me how much you love every last fucking inch of me." Her hips rise from the seat, rocking to meet my demanding thrusts as I nip along her neck. She's so fucking close. *Fuck, I'm so fucking close.* Her tits heave so hard against the tight neckline of her dress as she takes me, I half expect them to spill from it.

"Are you going to make a mess of your husband?" I taunt as she hovers at the edge of her release.

"Yes," she pants, clawing at my shirt. "And I want him to make a mess of me."

"Fuck!" I groan, slamming into her. *If my dirty little wife wants to be dripping with cum, who am I to refuse?* "I couldn't deny your request if I tried."

Picking up my pace, I savagely slam my cock into her cunt. Her legs wrap around my waist, pulling me deeper with every thrust until she falls apart beneath me. She comes so fucking hard that she squeezes around my cock like a vise, and it's my undoing.

I come with a roar, my cock twitching as I spill myself into her. Gripping the base of my cock, I pull from her and shoot a ribbon of cum across her pussy. I rub my hand through it and smear it over her swollen lips, making a mess of her just as she asked.

Being careful not to disturb my mess, I carefully pull her panties back into place and lower her dress. I wipe my cum-covered hand across my boxer briefs, tuck myself back into them, and pull up my trousers. Climbing onto the seat beside my beautiful, flushed bride, I place a soft kiss against her lips. Catlin struggles to catch her breath as we approach the reception hall, no longer looking quite as put together as she was when she walked into the church on Conor's arm.

"I look forward to enjoying our reception knowing that you're covered in me and I'm dripping down your thighs," I whisper, slipping out of the back of the limo to help her from it and onto her unsteady legs. I pull her tightly to me and kiss up her neck, pressing my lips to her ear. "But not nearly as much as I look forward to cleaning you up when we get home."

EPILOGUE
CATLIN

While I am standing in the very spot I had envisioned when I moved from Galway to New York a little over a three years ago, things are so different from what I imagined. This isn't how I expected my life to turn out.

Standing on the stage and waiting to receive my diploma from New York University, I stare into the crowd at my family. Finn, who has been nothing but supportive as I labored through grueling finals and countless late nights of writing papers to get here. Sitting to his right, his brothers and my new sisters gazing up at me as they wait to celebrate my accomplishment.

And on Finn's left is Uncle Sean, clutching my husband's hand as he beams at me with teary, pride-filled eyes.

A divine miracle is the only way to explain the two of them having grown so close.

"Catlin O'Flaherty-Evans." My name pours through the speakers, and my family erupts with cheers and applause. The outlandishly obnoxious kind you see in videos online as Fiona proudly waves her sign in the air. *Congratulations, Auntie Catlin!*

It definitely isn't the life I pictured, but there isn't a thing about I would change. That loud, foul-mouthed, sarcastic bunch are my family, and I couldn't imagine my life without them.

While I'm talking to my friends after the ceremony, I spot Finn weaving through the crowd to get to me. He pulls me into him and presses his lips to mine, kissing me hard and deep. *Like how he loves me.* Cupping my face, he stares down at me and purrs, "I'm so fucking proud of you, *piscín.*"

"We're all so proud of you," Liam chimes. "I just don't think we're all going to show you quite like that."

"Speak for yourself." Conor teasingly pushes himself between me and Finn.

"You're just trying to get yourself in trouble, aren't you?" I put my hands on his chest and shove him away.

Finn drapes his arm around my shoulders and holds me against him as we all make our way toward the parking lot. He helps me into the front seat of his Audi and reaches in to clip my seatbelt. His lips dust against mine, and he insists, "I really am fucking proud of you. After dinner with this lot, I intend you show how much."

Dinner is loud and obnoxious—as it always is with my family—and everyone slowly excuses themselves as it starts to get late. By the time Finn and I walk from the now-closing restaurant, the streetlights are on and the sky has grown dark.

Lacing his fingers with mine, we cross the street and walk into Central Park. We leisurely stroll around the lake, talking about everything and nothing. Finn glances at his watch and squeezes my hand. "We should probably head home, *piscín*. It's getting late."

Pulling myself into his arm, I stare up at him and flirtatiously rebut, "It isn't *that* late."

Finn lets out a deep chuckle as he grips my chin. Tipping my face toward his, he places a soft kiss against my lips. When he pulls back, he gravelly whispers, "Then you better fucking *run*."

 I take off with a giggle—happy that I switched into Converse from my heels after the graduation ceremony—as I sprint through the grass and toward the trees. Glancing over my shoulder when I reach the tree line, he's already on my heels.

"You know you can't outrun me," he shouts, closing the distance between us.

I know he's right, and I can't.

I *never* can.

Not that I ever really want to.

Ducking behind a large oak tree, I try to hide as I hear him getting close.

"I can hear you breathing. Your heart is fucking racing," he taunts. "Is it with excitement or fear, knowing that when I catch you, I'm going to take what's mine?"

Cupping my hands over my mouth, I try to muffle my increasingly heavy breaths as he stalks closer.

He's so close.

"You know you can't hide from me. You could run to the farthest corners of the earth." His voice gets deeper as he gets closer to me. He can't be more than a few feet away. "But the sweet aroma of your dripping cunt will always lead me right to you."

 I scream as he reaches around my hiding spot and roughly grabs my wrist. Futilely, I try to pull away from him, but he easily overpowers me and pins me to the cool grass as he climbs between my thighs. Pulling my panties to the side, he sinks into me as he grunts, "Mine."

Wrapping my legs around his hips, I pull him deeper into me. "Always."

ACKNOWLEDGMENTS

First, I would like to thank Katie (again), for the pep talks as I struggled and helping me to find my words so I could pour them into Finn & Catlin's story. More than anything, thank you for pushing me to be better with every word we publish together.

Thank you to Amanda for being my late night sounding board, an amazing alpha reader and my friend. You have no idea how much your love and support means to me or has helped.

Thank you to LO for coordinating my chaos so that I can focus on the words.

As always, love and thanks to my amazingly supportive husband—even if his support is secretly fueled with the hope I can retire him, so he can play golf everyday. *I'm wise to your plan.*

Last but definitely not least, thank you to my readers and my support teams, because without all of you, none of this would be possible.

ALSO BY J.L. QUICK

THE MEN OF CLUB TRISKELION SERIES

- Owned
- Bound
- Primal
- Master (Coming February 2025)
- Shared (Coming April 2025)
- Daddy (Coming May 2025)

THE SAVAGELY DEPRAVED SERIES

- Dark Devils
- Family Ties
- Wicked Love
- Brutal Bond

THE BOTTICELLI BROTHERHOOD SERIES

- Sold to the Syndicate
- Capo Dei Capi's Daughter
- Indebted to the Enemy
- Falling for the Mafia Dom

THE MARCANO MOGULS SERIES

- Tryst
- Crave
- Intern
- Savage

www.ingramcontent.com/pod-product-compliance
Lightning Source LLC
Chambersburg PA
CBHW071151100726
47908CB00002B/328